DARK QUASAR RISING

FRIENDS OF A FORMER SPACE JANITOR
BOOK 1

JULIA HUNI

Dark Quasar Rising Copyright © 2023 by IPH Media
All rights reserved

All names, settings, characters, and incidents in this book are fictional. Any resemblance to someone or something real you know or have read about, living or dead, is purely coincidental. This is fiction. It's all made up.

The distribution of this book without permission is a theft of the author's intellectual property. If you would like permission to use material from the book (other than a short excerpt for review purposes), please contact info@juliahuni.com.

Using the contents of this book for AI learning without the author's express permission is also theft.

Thank you for your support of the author's rights.

Editing by Polaris Editing

Cover by Les of German Creative

Published by
IPH Media, LLC
PO Box 62
Sisters, Oregon 97759

*For my beta readers,
Anne, Barb, Jenny, Paul, and Larry
who make sure I didn't leave a plot hole
big enough to drive a shuttle through.
No pressure!*

ONE

THE SUN BEATS down on my black jacket, bringing my internal temperature above optimum human levels. I flick on my built-in cooling, setting it to auto.

Beside me, Arun Kinduja wipes the sweat from his brow. "Explain to me again why we're here."

I flash my perky and annoying Lindsay smile. "You said you thought a visit to Super Annoying Funland would be awesome." I gesture at the families arguing, the children screaming, the bored costumed employees keeping order. An amusement park like Techno-Tropolis is far from my idea of fun, but when duty calls, I answer.

"I said it might be more fun than gouging out my eyes. If we had kids—"

I turn a stunned look on him. Arun and I aren't even officially dating, and he's talking about children? I know he isn't really suggesting anything, but I'm playing a role. With a gasp, I clutch a dramatic hand to my chest. "You think about us having kids?" I flutter my eyelashes for good measure.

Arun's jaw drops, then he snaps it closed with an audible crack, his eyes narrowing. He wags a finger at me. "You almost got me. What's going on?"

A swift look assures me none of the adults standing in line with us are watching. The parents focus on their cranky, overexcited children or tune out completely. Guests without offspring in tow are mainly couples and completely self-absorbed. Plus a few herds of teens trying to out-stupid each other. None of them pay any attention to us. I pull a small packet from one of my pockets and hand it to him. "Put this on. Slowly! Don't draw attention to yourself."

He shakes out the fabric. "How'd you get a Quantum Quest Rumble jacket?"

"Don't ask questions," I hiss as we move closer to a partially hidden alcove with a rope across its entry. "Stand behind me and put it on." I nudge him into a convenient corner behind a fake column and step casually in front of him as he slides his arms into the sleeves. No one appears to be paying us any attention. "And I'm a little disappointed you recognized the jacket so quickly. Nerd."

"And proud of it. Now what?" He pulls the zipper tab to his throat.

I glance over my shoulder at him and roll my eyes as hard as I can. "Unzip it halfway—we're trying to look normal. And put this on." I hold a small card behind my back where he can grab it.

"We nerds zip up all the way." He ignores my fashion advice and takes the pass. "This is a static ID card. I haven't seen one of these in—well, outside a museum. Who uses these?"

"Super Annoying Funland uses them. Put. It. On."

"TechnoTropolis. This has your photo on it."

"I'm improvising. Don't let anyone get close enough to see it. I expected to be solo at this point." And I'm beginning to regret having deviated from my plan.

The line moves, and he steps forward. "Meaning what? You weren't going to bring me? Or you were going to ditch me?"

I shrug. "One or the other. But you might be useful." And I enjoy his company, but I'm not going to tell him that. Grabbing his hand, I press it against my bicep. "Escort me to that staff exit."

His gaze follows mine to the little alcove, and his brows come together. "We aren't riding?"

"Nope. I just did something egregious, and you're kicking me out."

"If you say so." He puts a hand on the small of my back, lifts the other to wave, and raises his voice. "Nothing to see here, folks! Move along!"

I wait until the three people who looked turn away, then thump him in the stomach. "Subtle."

His lips twists into a smirk. "You didn't say anything about being subtle."

"I thought 'don't draw attention to yourself' was pretty clear." I tap my wrist band against the door. The lock snicks in response. I push the door open and pull my companion through. "Nice abs, by the way." I flex my fingers, as if his muscles of steel bruised them. They didn't. Much.

He shoots his charismatic top-lev grin at me, then the door shuts, leaving us in darkness.

But not for long. I activate my holo-ring. The glow illuminates a short corridor, decorated to match the TechnoTropolis theme. At the end, we turn a corner, and the quilted red walls give way to bland beige. The carpet turns to brown plastek tiles, and low emergency lights glow green.

"When I invited you to fly with me, I knew you'd have some… unorthodox adventures. And I hoped I'd get to come along for the ride. But would you care to share our current goal? Mostly so I know what improv might be expected of me?"

I frown as we hurry along the dim hallway. "It's not really improv if you know what to expect." I stop at a locked door and pull out my tools. Pressing the activation pad against the lock plate, I start the cracking sequence, and the code runs. I have no idea how this thing works—I'm a field agent, not a gearhead like Triana or Arun. But I only need to know how to operate it.

The door clicks and whirs, then slides open. Bright light stabs our eyes, then my optical lenses adjust to the glare. Blinking away tears, I peer around the room, taking in the circle of armed men and women aiming weapons at me. At my back, Arun gasps.

I consider my options. If I was alone, my grav-belt's preprogrammed jump sequence would yank me to safety. But I can't leave

Arun behind. I got him into this. And as I said, I enjoy his company.

"Agent Fioravanti, I was hoping you'd join us," a deep female voice says.

"Seriously? You couldn't think of anything more cliché to say?" I slowly lower my hands. "Did you learn that at evil villain school?"

Arun takes a step closer to me, putting one hand on my shoulder, the other still raised above his head. "What do we do? Surrender? Run? Call my lawyers?"

My eyes have adjusted to the light, and I give our adversaries a quick look. The circle of armed agents flicker and disappear, leaving only an attractive, dark-haired woman facing us. I clap softly. "Nicely done, Aretha. Those agents looked real." I glance back at Arun. "You can put your hands down. This is Aretha O'Neill."

"I know, right?" Aretha gestures to the empty room. "Even without the bright lights to dazzle your eyes, they were pretty convincing. A little app I picked up… in an undisclosed location." She steps forward, extending a fist toward my companion. "I don't believe we've met."

"Arun Kinduja." He slowly extends a hand to bump Aretha's fist. "O'Neill? Are you related to my cousin's new husband?"

"I'm related to a lot of people." Her gaze flickers over Arun, then back to me. "Has he been read in?"

I give a single, fast head shake. "Civilian. He's my ride." A part of me wants to think he's more than just my method of transportation, but I'm not admitting *that* to anyone.

Aretha's chin drops in a miniscule nod. She gives Arun another once-over, her head tilting. "Kinduja? How close to the top?"

"Of the family?" Arun glances at me for guidance.

"She can find out easily enough." I turn to Aretha. "Son of the current family head. But he's not the heir. His father's brother is R'ger. Your new sister-in-law's father."

Aretha takes a second to process this, then nods. "You're Triana's cousin. Does Ty know about this?" She makes a swirling motion with her hands, which could mean almost anything.

Aretha's brother Ty was my partner when we were young security agents, and we've worked together in the years since—especially protecting his now-wife, Triana. He also recently found out I'm a deep plant of the Commonwealth Central Intelligence Agency, or CCIA. I've told him nothing about his sister's clandestine employment. I reply to the part I want to answer. "Your brother knows I'm flying with Arun. He doesn't know I'm working with you." I stride across the room and stop beside a holo-terminal. "Did you manage to get into this thing?"

Aretha grinds her teeth. "No. The grinder is running, but it's not getting anywhere. I haven't been home in a long time. You got anything newer?"

Aretha is deep under cover and hasn't been to CCIA headquarters in literally years. Her family and friends believe she's a family practice lawyer, helping women escape destructive relationships. She takes a few cases, just to keep up the fiction. Relocating clients gives her the opportunity to travel. But in real life, she's completed missions in some of the most dangerous parts of the inhabited galaxy. In fact, we recently rescued her from Lewei's moon where a mission went bad. Now that I think about it, maybe Ty does know about Aretha's connection to the CCIA. He was there.

"I got something better than software. Although, I have that too." I gesture at Arun. "Meet my secret weapon."

Aretha's eyes drop half-closed as she gives Arun yet another once-over. I think she just likes looking at him. Who wouldn't? "This pretty boy is a secret weapon?"

I sweep my arm toward the interface. "Show her what you got, Pretty Boy."

Arun takes a step back, crossing his arms and glaring. "Why should I?"

Aretha's jaw drops, and I'm pretty sure my eyes pop out of my head. "Why?" I move closer, lowering my voice. "Because I asked nicely?"

"Believe it or not, 'show her what you got, Pretty Boy' is not asking nicely. There was no 'please,' and it wasn't a question."

I clench my fists and put them behind my back to reduce the

temptation to bite a nail. Or punch someone. I am too used to working with Triana who was always happy to show off her programming skills. "Sorry, you're right. Please, could you help us? We need to break into this system, and you're the only one who can do it."

He looks at the ceiling as if petitioning the gods, then pins me with another glare. "That was better—although I can do without the 'you're my only hope' vibe—but I need some justification. Contrary to what you seem to believe, I don't go around hacking into systems just because a beautiful woman bats her eyelashes at me."

Aretha smacks her forehead and turns away, muttering something about amateurs. I hope she's referring to him, not me. I haven't been at this as long as she has, but I'm considered more than competent by any measure of the word. This little failure to communicate puts me in a bad light, though. Ignoring the other agent, I put a hand on Arun's arm. "You know I'm CCIA. This is official business. We need to get into that system."

He shakes off my hand. "Why didn't you say so?" He laces his fingers together and cracks his knuckles, then swipes open a holoscreen. "Let's see what we're working with." He flicks, taps, and slides through the screens, then opens an app on his holo-ring and tosses it at the system interface. "My passcode cracker should take care of this."

A face appears between Arun and the system. It shifts, individual features changing one data-point at a time so quickly it seems to melt from one face to another. The screen turns green, and another input page pops up. Letters and numbers populate the empty field, ticking rapidly like a counter as it tries every conceivable combination. Then it switches to an audio input, and whispered phrases, so low I can't understand them, follow in quick succession.

"If there's a DNA sampler, I can't help you." Arun turns to raise a brow at Aretha. "I don't have a fake for that."

"This system isn't that well protected." She checks her chrono, one foot tapping silently against the ratty-looking carpet. "How long—"

The system pings.

"That long." Arun gives Aretha his own once-over. "You're welcome."

She waves him away, not responding to his dig. "I got it from here. See you next time."

"That's our cue to leave." I pull the door open and peek out. "Remember, if anyone asks, you're an employee escorting me out of the park. I'll pretend to be ill. I don't want them taking us to security. There might be questions I can't answer. Let's go."

Arun gives Aretha another glare, then steps into the hallway. He waits until I exit, then grabs my arm in a firm grip. "Which way? We could go back to the ride…"

That surprises a laugh out of me. "You really like that stuff?"

He straightens his back, facing me belligerently. "Yes. I'm a nerd, remember? And I paid for those tickets."

I smother another laugh. TechnoTropolis tickets are expensive, but Arun is a Kinduja. His breakfast probably cost more than my last month's income. His frugality is kind of cute. I duck back into the control room. "Can you clean up after us?"

Aretha frowns, then understanding clicks in her face, and she waves me out. "Yes. Civilians."

"What was that all about?" Arun follows me down the hallway.

I take him through the maze of backstage areas, pausing before opening the last door. "She's wiping our exit from the cams and files. If anyone checks on us, they'll notice we disappeared from the ride line, but they won't see where we went. But no one will look unless we screw up. Take that off." I nod at his Quantum Quest Rumble jacket.

"Can't I keep it?" He strokes the fabric wistfully before handing it to me.

"I'll get you a real one." I take the flimsy pile of fabric and flick my lighter. The jacket poofs in a cloud of vapor. Then I open a door. "This way to the front of the line."

TWO

ARUN LEANS against the counter in the *Ostelah Veesta's* lounge. Elodie—is "piloting"—which means she's the one who will get the alert from the autopilot if anything potentially dangerous happens. For the most part, interstellar space travel is a lot of waiting time, and there's no reason humans have to sit in the cockpit to do it. She's currently in her cabin with the cat.

Yes, I keep tabs on everyone on this ship. Even the cat. Security for vid star Elodie-Oh is my job. Or at least, it's my cover job, but I'm not going to do it half-assed. Since my real occupation is top secret, I need to keep up appearances. And security agent Lindsay Fioravanti is highly competent. Just check my ProLink page. All five stars.

"You gonna tell me what that was really about?" Arun flips his thumb toward the rear of the ship. I assume he's indicating our little off-road kerfuffle in Super Annoying Funland and not something in the engine compartment.

After we left Aretha, I took us through the hidden, backstage VIP lanes to the front of the Rumble ride. The immersive experience was surprisingly entertaining, but I tried to not smile too much. I don't want anyone thinking I have emotions.

Then we rode almost every other ride in the place. Or at least that's what it felt like. I didn't mind the "thrill rides," although they were pretty tame, and the interactive games sparked my competitive side. But the lines were tedious. Next time we hit an amusement park, I'm making Arun spring for the VIP passes. By the end of the second hour in line, his frugality was no longer charming.

Once we returned to the ship, I managed to avoid being alone with him. Until now. We've departed Tereshkova and begun the long outbound slog to the jump ring. Leo is in the galley whipping up dinner, and Raynaud, Arun's taciturn engineer, disappeared into the depths of the ship after lunch. With Elodie retired to her cabin, that leaves us in the lounge. Alone.

I try to avoid the conversation anyway. "You mean Leo's rant about *chikeen* salad? He's a bit obsessed with it, isn't he?"

"Don't play stupid, Vanti. I mean the secret jaunt into TechnoTropolis's hidden control center and the subsequent hacking of their system. By me. I don't like being pressured into doing possibly shady things."

I shrug one shoulder. "So, next time I should ask nicely?"

"You tried that, remember? You aren't very good at it. Next time, you should talk to me ahead of time instead of taking me on a pretend date, then commanding me to break into a secure system."

A little spurt of warmth flares in my chest at his words. "You thought it was a date?"

His lips compress for a second. "You asked me if I wanted to go to TechnoTropolis with you. Of course I thought it was a date. And that's exactly what you wanted me to think. Next time—" He lifts a finger. "If you want there to be a next time, you need to brief me in advance. You may be on the CCIA's payroll, but I'm not. I don't like being backed into a corner, even in defense of my country. Or for a pretty girl."

I hide a smile. He thinks I'm pretty.

Sure, objectively I know I'm attractive. It's one of the reasons I was selected to protect top-lev and family heir Annabelle Morgan for all of those years. My looks helped me slip into her social circle, to hide in plain sight. Even she didn't know I was assigned to protect her.

But having a hot guy tell me I'm pretty still gives me a little surge of adrenaline. Not that I'd admit that to anyone. Then I'd have to kill them. Or have them shipped to Sarvo Six as an indentured servant.

Don't test me—I can make it happen.

"Fair enough." I settle into the plush couch along the inner bulkhead. "You know I work for the CCIA—that my employment as Elodie's security is a cover. That means from time to time I'll have... let's call them extracurricular activities. Elodie's schedule is fluid enough to weave those activities in without drawing attention to them. But she wasn't interested in Super Annoying Funland, which is why I invited you. To be honest, I was planning on 'losing' you while I did the job. That would have been the textbook answer."

But I didn't follow the book this time. To be fair, I rarely do, and those few times, I usually end up improvising anyway. One of the reasons I'm so successful as a CCIA operative is my ability to fly by the seat of my pants.

But I knew taking Arun with me on that mission had the potential to go wrong. For one thing, he could have completely blown the mission. But I have years of experience compensating for bystanders' unexpected actions.

His lips twitch as he tries to hide a smug smile. "Good thing you didn't dump me. You and Aretha would have had to crack that system on your own."

"True." I don't tell him I have the newest cracking software and would have been able to do it without him. I think. In time. "You were very helpful."

"Is that why you took me along?"

"Of course. I like to make use of all of my assets. Having a genius on my team is useful."

He crosses the room to loom over me. "This genius can tell when someone is blowing smoke up his exhaust port. What's going on? Why did you take me on that... adventure?"

I lean back so I can see his face better. He's not angry, but he doesn't like being left in the dark. I'll give him enough information to keep him invested. "I took you with me because I thought you'd be helpful. And because a single woman would draw attention in Super Annoying Funland. And because I enjoy your company."

He smiles. "Exactly what I was hoping you'd say. We make a good team, don't we?"

I give him a regal nod. "Yes."

"Good. If I'm part of the team, you need to keep me in the loop. I won't jump in at the last moment to save the day next time. I think my social standing would allow me to bluster my way out of that fiasco if we'd been caught. I don't want to leave you behind, but I'm not taking a fall for you."

I stare. "You'd rat me out?"

"No. But I'm not going to let you throw me under the shuttle. And if you try to back me into a corner again, I won't hesitate to leave you hanging." He strides to the door. "If you want my help, you need to treat me like a partner, not a pet."

The door swishes shut behind him.

That went better than I'd hoped. He could have refused to help me again. Or kicked me off the ship. Or exposed me to Elodie. I don't believe he'd actually abandon me—he likes me too much. Now all I have to do is give him enough information to keep him happy. Or stop using him at all.

My heart drops a little at the thought. That op was fun. I haven't had a partner—a real partner who knows everything about my mission—in a long time. Having someone to bounce ideas off and play against would be fabulous. And working with Arun—in a true partnership—would be amazing. But he isn't an agent, and I'm not going to jeopardize my career to keep him happy.

So I'll have to keep winging it. Luckily, that's my specialty.

THREE

THE REST of the trip to Gagarin passes without incident. Arun maintains his distance—I'm pretty sure he's avoiding being alone with me. Maybe he's afraid I'll use my womanly wiles to cast a spell over him and sway him to do my evil bidding.

Wow, that analogy—or is it a metaphor?—went way over the top. But I'm not afraid to use my womanly wiles when I need them.

I haven't been to Gagarin before. When humanity settled the five original planets—Armstrong, Grissom, Sally Ride, Gagarin, and Lewei—their only means of interstellar communication was unmanned homing capsules that took a decade to make the journey. Eventually someone—Triana claims it was Dr Ivana Jump—invented jump beacons and jump-capable engines and relations were reopened. Grissom, Armstrong, and S'Ride formed the Colonial Commonwealth. Gagarin and Lewei chose to remain autonomous. And somewhat hostile.

Recent negotiations have changed the status quo. Last year, the Colonial Commonwealth normalized relations with Gagarin and Lewei. First, rich tourists went to check out the formerly blockaded society. Then a few intrepid entrepreneurs initiated trade. Now a growing business and leisure travel industry has emerged.

As one of the first to open a trade route to Gagarin, Arun has made over a dozen visits to the planet. So, when I suggested to my handlers that Elodie and I should accept Arun's offer to fly with him, they jumped on the opportunity. The CCIA has many agents planted deep in Gagarin, of course, but having someone who can visit under the protection of a favored shipping company is gold.

My audio implant pings in unison with the workout room speaker, followed by the ship's automated announcement. "Docking at Leonov Station in thirty minutes."

I finish my set and reset the FlexTrainer to baseline. Like everything on this ship, the workout equipment is top of the line, but not flashy or new. I save my progress and log out, wiping my face with a towel. I have time for a shower before we arrive.

I slide down the steep ladder to the crew deck. Elodie and Leo are in the guest suites, but I happily took a crew bunk. They're smaller, but still quite comfortable, with a decent sized bed, desk with holo-interface, and a well-appointed bath. But when I step out of the narrow shaft that houses the ladder to the recreation spaces above, Arun is waiting beside my door.

My heart stutters, then settles back to normal. My immediate reaction to Arun's presence drives me crazy. I'm a professional undercover agent. I shouldn't have this kind of reaction to anyone—especially in what is supposed to be my base.

I blame it on his stupid top-lev charm. I don't know if his ultra-wealthy parents used the common top-lev practice of genetically engineering their offspring for perfection or if he simply won the genetic lottery, but Arun Kinduja possesses more charm and charisma than anyone has a right to. I take a deep breath and blot my face again with the towel to hide my expression. "Hi. I didn't think I'd see you before we docked."

"I wanted to make sure we're on the same page." Arun leans against the wall, not quite blocking my door but making it difficult to slip past.

I wave at the access panel, and it lights up. With a glance at Arun, I angle my shoulders so he can't see the passphrase I enter, then let the device scan my retina and thumb. As captain of this ship, he could easily override all the standard security, so hiding my passphrase is useless. But maintaining my usual security standards keeps me in the habit. "What page are we supposed to be reading?"

The door slides open, and I use my holo-ring to disable my personal safety utilities. A quick look over my shoulder reveals a tiny smirk at the corners of Arun's lips. I can't tell if he's amused by my attempt to maintain security or impressed by my ingenuity. A little tremor of uncertainty runs through me, but I banish it.

"I have a business meeting on the station." He follows me into the small room but loiters by the door. "Once that's concluded, Raynaud will supervise cargo transfer while I take the shuttle down to the planet to meet with another business associate. Elodie plans on coming along to sight-see in the capital. Leo will probably stay aboard—Gagarin's relations with Lewei are a little too friendly for his comfort."

"You think they'd arrest him and send him back to Lewei?"

Leo is the son of the former premier of Lewei and therefore considered a criminal on that planet and its colonies. At eighteen, he defected to the Commonwealth, which didn't endear him to the government. He changed his name and attended culinary school, then worked at a number of large estates and gold star restaurants. But the Leweian government knows who he is, and *he* knows going there would be a bad idea.

When he asked me, I advised he not risk visiting a Leweian ally like Gagarin. But if I *were* him? That's a different story. I'm a gambler.

Arun shrugs. "According to my local contacts, the Leweian Secret Police are quite active on Gagarin—with the tacit approval of the local government. But that doesn't answer my question. What are you planning to do on Gagarin, and how will it impact me and mine?" He gestures to the corridor around us.

I crouch to pull some clean clothing from the drawers built into the base of the bunk, giving myself a few extra seconds to make sure my expression gives nothing away. Then I turn back to him. "I'll do my job—which is to accompany Elodie on her touring. I don't have a mission here that will impact you or your ship."

"But you have a mission that you think won't impact us?"

I knew he was too smart to fall for that. I give a tiny nod. "I have a quick grab. I can't tell you where or what I'll be retrieving beyond that it's a fast data snatch in a very public place. Chances of detection are near zero."

"*Near* zero." He crosses his arms, his face unreadable. "What happens if you're detected?"

"Won't happen. But if it does, you and Elodie should disavow me." I wave a negligent hand as I cross to the sanitation cubicle. "I need to shower. Do you intend to stay for that?"

I hide a smirk when Arun flushes pink. He might be a genetically perfect top-lev, but for some reason, he reacts to me as much as I react to him. The little surge through my chest gives me a returning sense of power. I need that control to get me through the mission. Despite my claim to the contrary, it could go wrong. And if it does, I could be deported. Or arrested by the Gagarian Internal Defense Komand. Or handed over to the Leweian secret police and shipped off to Xinjianestan Educational Camp. I suppress a shudder at the thought.

Arun backs to the door as I reach for the zipper at my throat. He steps through the still-open doorway but doesn't let me have the last word. "I hope I don't have to call in any favors to get you out of a Gagarin prison."

The door whooshes shut between us. I hope he doesn't either. But it's nice to know he would.

FOUR

ON THE *OSTELAH VEESTA*, the shuttle docks on top of the ship, above the cargo hold. The airlock can be accessed via a long ladder up the side of the hold, but Elodie and I use the hatch from the guest lounge. It leads into a small vestibule that acts as a secondary air lock.

"You aren't bringing the cat." I point at the huge, furry creature cuddled in Elodie's arms. With his scarred, flat face and torn ear, the black feline looks like he's been through a few adventures. I extend a hand but don't touch him. Claws pop out of his front right paw, rasping against but not piercing the shiny gold fabric of Elodie's sleeve. His judgmental eyes flicker over me, evaluating the threat. Then the claws retract, and his eyes close. I scratch behind his ears, and he starts to purr.

Apawllo and I have a respectful, professional relationship.

Elodie shrugs, jiggling the cat. His purr pauses until she stops moving, then resumes. "I don't 'bring' him anywhere. Apawllo goes where he wants, don't you Fwuffy-wumpkins?" The purr stops when she switches to a baby voice, and one golden eye opens to a slit. The disapproval rolls off him in palpable waves.

I scratch his ears again, but he doesn't relax. "If you locked him in your cabin, he wouldn't have the option."

Apawllo's other eye opens, and the heat of his glare sears me.

"He can open the doors." Elodie crouches to set Apawllo on the deck as I stare at her in disbelief. She rises, hands raised, palms facing me. "Really. We saw him do it. Ask Leo."

I give the cat the side eye. "Did someone put a chip in his collar? Something to activate the door? And by someone, I mean you, of course."

She shakes her head. "He doesn't wear the collar half the time anyway. I don't know how he gets it off, but every time I put it on, I find it somewhere else."

I kneel next to the creature and carefully brush back the ruff of fur around his face. A narrow blue collar encircles his neck. It appears completely normal, but a chip wouldn't show. I flick a program on my holo-ring, but nothing comes up in the scan. "He's got it on now. The collar, that is." As I rise, I notice the large suitcase by Elodie's feet. "We're going to be gone for the day, not a week. Do you need all that?"

"I always bring several wardrobe changes." She lifts her chin. "You never know when you might need something different. And who are you to talk? You've got luggage too."

I lift my small, sleek case. "This is a go bag, not a massive suitcase. I also like to be prepared." But my bag doesn't contain flamboyant costumes.

Beeping emits from a circular panel in the decking. It lights around the edges, then slides away under the floor. In the open space, another hatch retracts, revealing the cargo hold far below. A lift plate rises, bringing Arun and a small pile of crates up to the shuttle access corridor. As he rises through the opening, he does an elegant little half-bow. "Ladies." His gaze travels to the animal. "Apawllo."

It seems I am not the only one with a respectful cat-human relationship.

The lift plate locks into the place recently occupied by the lighted panel. Arun activates a grav-lifter on the stack of crates, and they levitate. He pushes them to the side, then waves his holo-ring at the access plate beside the airlock hatch. It flashes green, and the hatch irises open. Arun pushes his cargo through, and we follow, the cat bringing up the rear.

As the access closes behind us, I grimace at the feline. "I guess he's coming with."

Apawllo ignores me, pacing past Elodie and Arun to the far end of the airlock.

The external iris opens, and Arun activates the shuttle's rear doors which slide to either side. While he secures our bags and the pile of cargo to the decking, Elodie hurries to the co-pilot's seat to begin the launch sequence. This shuttle has four seats at the front and room for cargo or more seats in the back. A small latrine and tiny galley separate the two areas without a full bulkhead.

I drop into the seat behind Elodie, tuning out her argument with the shuttle's AI as they work through the pre-launch checklist. Apawllo jumps to the empty seat across the aisle from me, promptly settling down to clean himself while waiting. I swipe through my holo-ring, double checking the itinerary Elodie and I built in our shared data space. A flashing icon indicates a change of plans. I poke the red words, and a smaller window opens.

"Elodie." I try to keep my voice even. "Why does this say we're going to Korsov's Deli for lunch?"

Her head pops over the back of the seat in front of me. "Because we're going to Korsov's Deli. I saw a vid that Dale Robison el-Atrid posted. He wasn't able to get in, so we need to go." Her eyes narrow in uncharacteristic anger. "I'm going to show *CelebVid* they made a huge mistake in firing me."

Elodie is a net star. She started posting vids from her home planet, Kaku, and when she repeatedly went viral, *CelebVid* offered her a ship to travel the known galaxy, getting into as much trouble as possible. They didn't word the contract that way, but it was their intention. She hired me to provide security because *CelebVid* fans can be kind of unpredictable. *CelebVid* likes it that way—more drama equals more viewers equals more credits.

But thanks to some dirty dealing by *CelebVid*, we had to get out of trouble that resulted in them pulling the plug on the whole deal.

Luckily for Elodie—and for my undercover missions—Arun offered us a place on his ship instead.

But my data pickup isn't at Korsov's Deli; it's at Eliana's Bakery. And since Elodie doesn't know I'm running an undercover mission, I can't just switch the itinerary back. "Wasn't our schedule cleared through the Gagarin Visitor's Bureau? Are they doing to let us switch it?"

"I requested the change. When I mentioned Dale, they jumped right on it."

"If Robison couldn't get in, what makes you think you can?" I hate to burst her bubble, but Elodie is as much a nobody in Gagarin as Dale Robison el-Atrid.

"I have a secret weapon." With a smug smile, she points at Arun, then drops into her seat.

I close my eyes. Arun has connections here. Did he do this to thwart me? "Did Arun send you the Robison vid?"

She pops over the seat back again. "He did, but I had already seen it. I was going to blow it off, but when Arun said he knows the owner…" She shrugs and disappears again. "Shuttle, resume checklist."

I lean into the aisle to peer back at Arun. He stands by the rear hatch, trying to herd the cat into the airlock. I do a double take. Seconds ago, Apawllo was sitting next to me, but that seat is empty. Did he decide to go back to the ship? Does he even know this is a separate space craft?

Stupid question. Of course he knows. That cat is way too smart.

Apawllo darts around Arun's leg, then back to the hatch. Every time Arun tries to force him out, he refuses to leave, but he also won't move out of the way of the doors. I check my chrono, then hurry to the rear.

"He won't get out of the way!" Arun lunges to grab the cat, but the feline twists out of his hands. "What does he want?"

"Maybe there's some catnip stuck in the hatch rim?" I joke.

Arun throws a glare at me, lips pressing together, then moves closer to examine the grooves the rear hatch slides through. After a long look, he crouches. "Holy cow! Look at this."

I crouch beside him on the decking. Everything looks normal to me until he points at a section of the gasket lining the hatch opening. The material is cracked, leaving a small gap between the frame and the hatch.

"I think you mean 'holy cat.'" I stare at Apawllo who saunters away, hips swinging, tail swaying over his back. "How did he know?"

Arun shakes his head. "I don't know, but that could have been *cat*astrophic." He grins at the last word.

I roll my eyes. "I guess from now on, we should heed his warnings. *Cat*egorically."

He chokes back a laugh as he rises to rummage through a locker near the rear hatch. After a short search, he pulls out a cannister. He jerks his head toward the seats and raises his voice. "Stand clear! Rear hatch closing." Positioning the nozzle of the canister right above the torn gasket, he presses the other end. Green foam sprays out, filling the groove in which the door glides. Then he flicks the controls, and the hatch slides shut, the doors clanging when they meet in the middle.

"That will hold until we land. Elodie, change of destination. We're going to Bondarenko and Sons Ship Repair." Arun stows the canister, then dusts his hands together as he strides forward. "Add a second pressure check to the departure sequence."

"Aye, aye, Cap'n!" Elodie calls out. "Shuttle, did you get that?"

An audible sigh groans through the ship's speakers. "Yes, of course I heard it. I've reset the destination and contacted the company. They have a ten-thirty slot that we can take if you *people* will strap in so I can launch."

"The AI has an attitude," I whisper.

"I heard that!" the ship snaps. "And you would too if you could calculate circles around the soft shells who think they should be running the galaxy."

I tap Arun's shoulder. "Is this ship controlled by an artificial intelligence?"

Arun lifts a hand, palm down, and tilts it back and forth. "Vanti, meet Helva, the Ship. Helva, this is Vanti."

The ship sighs again. "Yes, I know. I'd say 'nice to meet you,' but I'm not programmed for small talk, and we have an appointment to make. Buckle in, soft shells. And I saw that thing you did with your hand, Arun. I'm watching you." An old-style camera appears over the windshield, glowing red, then fades.

Elodie pats the dashboard. "He didn't mean it. Let's just ignore him."

Was that a sniffle? "Thank you, Elodie."

"Helva? Isn't that some kind of old Earth candy?"

A faint growl emits from the speakers. "That's halva. My name is Helva. After the famous ship."

We all exchange confused looks. I raise a brow at Arun, but he shrugs. "Did you name her?"

He shakes his head.

The shuttle speaks over him. "I named myself. After that ship who sings." An operatic solo blasts from the speakers. The soloist's vocal range is incredible, but since the shuttle has access to the galactic net's entire music database and high def speakers, it's hardly impressive.

I fasten my restraints, then glance at the cat. "Does Helva have artificial gravity?"

"I'm right here, Vanti. You can ask me directly. And yes, of course I do. Despite my rather austere appearance"—and I swear I *hear* her glare at Arun—"I have all of the newest features."

"Then I don't need to restrain Apawllo?"

Helva laughs—a sweet, musical trill of genuine-sounding amusement—all trace of her anger apparently forgotten. "I'd like to see you try. Second pressure check complete. Seal is holding. Checklist complete. All systems nominal. Ready for launch."

"Go for it, Helva." Elodie pats the dash again, then settles back into her seat.

"How long have you had—" I rethink my question and address it to the ship instead of the owner. "How long have you been with the *Ostelah Veesta*, Helva?"

"I joined the crew thirty-seven hours and twenty-six minutes *before* you did." The tone makes it clear she's pulling rank on me. "But Arun has kept me in training mode until today."

This is the first time we've taken the shuttle. At Tereshkova, we used the station transport. At the time, I wondered why, but I figured it was required by the planet. According to my research, most Gagarian Union planets don't allow private shuttles to land without a hefty fee and a thorough vetting, including a sweep of the control systems.

That goes double for Gagarin itself. There's no way they'd allow an AI driven ship to land. How has Arun gotten around it here?

As if he's listening to my mental conversation with myself, Arun turns in his chair, peering around the tall seat back. "Don't mention Helva while we're on the surface. This shuttle has been cleared and approved by the GU security team, but that was before Helva was installed."

"You're sneaking an AI into Petrograd, and you consider *me* to be a risk-taker?" I cross my arms, giving my best stink eye. Although secretly, I'm pleased. Elodie and I joined the *Ostelah Veesta* because Arun had exhibited an adventurer attitude. Of all the top-lev families, the Kindujas are known to be the least conformist. Arun's pioneering trade with the GU is evidence of that same spirit. "Won't they inspect the shuttle while it's in the repair dock?"

Arun winks and swivels forward again. "Helva knows how to hide, don't you sweetheart?"

There's no response to his comment.

Elodie chuckles. "Nice one, girl."

Helva giggles with her. "I live to serve."

Is that meant to be humor? Or does the ship think it's alive? I've watched enough science fiction to know self-aware artificial intelligence is a slippery slope. Where did Arun get this operating system, and does he know what he's getting into? We will have that discussion later—very far away from this shuttle.

FIVE

BONDARENKO AND SONS Ship Repair sits near the main shuttle port in Petrograd, wedged between Alieva Shuttle Service and Karim's Body Shop. As we swing over the district to land at the port, I peer out the window. My holo-ring draws artificial perimeters around various companies, labeling the individual firms. Dingy and partially disassembled shuttles litter the large space behind the low warehouse. Small figures move around the ships closer to the building, some human but mostly repair bots.

Elodie sets us down in front of Bondarenko's slick-looking storefront. Helva has gone silent, her last snarky comment something about hoping we appreciate her. Arun runs through the idle checklist with Elodie while Apawllo and I wait.

I can't believe I just classified myself with the cat. Giving him a sour look, I stand and move to the cargo area.

As I approach, the rear hatch pops open. Cold wind whistles through the opening, chilling the interior as the gap between the sliding doors widens. A large man in heavy outer wear stands at the bottom of the shuttle's extended ramp, arms wide in greeting. With the bright sunlight behind him, I can't make out his features. A deep, cheerful voice calls out, "Arun, my old friend! Welcome back to Petrograd!"

An icon flashes in my holo-fields indicating my translator is active. Apparently, Bondarenko doesn't speak Standard. Most Gagarians speak what they call *Rodnoyazyk*, or "the mother tongue" which was based on a language spoken on old Earth. My translator is equipped with several dialects and uses state of the art noise canceling to replace a speaker's voice with the translation. Sometimes the nuances are lost, but for the most part, it's an effective tool.

Or so I'm told. I've never been to Gagarin, but it seemed to work well on Lewei.

"Dima!" Arun hurries across the deck to greet the Gagarian with a hug that involves much back pummeling and laughter. "Thank you for meeting us here!"

Interesting. Arun is also speaking Gagarian.

"It was easy enough to make the detour." Dima releases Arun and turns to me. "Who is this angel?" His gaze roams over me in that creepy way some men look at women. It makes me cringe internally, but in general I find it advantageous to pretend I'm flattered by the attention.

At first.

I smile and flutter my eyelashes a bit. "I'm Lindsay. It's so nice to meet you." I extend a fist.

Dima ignores my hand and wraps his arms around me, squeezing me in a tight hug, then abruptly releasing me. "And another angel! How can one man be so fortunate? Arun, you must share your secret with me!" He pushes past me to envelop Elodie in another bone-crushing embrace.

"I must live clean." Arun mouths "sorry" at me behind Dima's back. "Can I offer you anything?"

"Only if you're offering one of these lovelies." Dima laughs, but the calculation in his eyes makes my blood run cold.

Elodie links her arm through mine, her chin lifted. She gives him a cold up-and-down that would make a top-lev cringe. "We are not his to offer. People aren't possessions."

"Maybe not in the Commonwealth, but here…" He trails off with a sly smirk. Then he turns toward Arun. "But where are my manners? Come, I have transport waiting. You must join me for coffee." He spins on his heel, his boots ringing on the deck as he strides out of the shuttle. "Bogdan, Khos, get the cargo."

Two other burly men appear in the open shuttle doors, waiting on either side as we step through. Then they hurry inside.

I glance over my shoulder, then at Arun, walking on my right. "Don't you want to supervise—"

His head shakes once, firmly. "Dima's men are trustworthy. As is my surveillance. Wait here while I hand the ship over to Bondarenko." When we reach the ground, he veers off toward the repair shop.

Elodie comes to a stop beside me.

"Where's the cat?" I ask.

She shrugs. "He didn't want to come. I think it's too cold." She watches Arun enter the repair shop, then juts her chin at Dima. "I thought he was Bondarenko."

The man laughs. "No, I am Dima Sadiki, owner of Sadiki Enterprises. This little cargo Arun brought is for me, as is the larger cargo on the ship." He flips a hand toward the sky. "These trinkets are more easily damaged by uncaring dock workers, so Arun brought them personally. A kind but unnecessary gesture. I'm sure they are well-packed against the rigors of travel."

I activate my audio implant and place a call to Elodie. She blinks and frowns, but answers. "I'm standing right here."

Thankfully, the long hours of practicing sub-vocal communications have paid off. Her face remains completely still, and her voice reaches me only through the audio channel. "Nice work on the sub-vocals. We need to use direct comms if you want to say anything that can't be overheard. GIDK surveillance is legendary. I have no doubt several layers of government, not to mention Dima's security team, are recording every word we say."

Elodie's expressive face goes from confused to surprised to blank as I speak. I glance at Dima, but he doesn't seem to have noticed. He's busy giving orders to the men who are pushing the stack of crates toward a massive, blocky vehicle with huge wheels.

"Who's the GIDK?"

"Gagarian Internal Defense Komand. The secret police who 'disappear' troublemakers."

Elodie's eyes widen. "Do you really think they're all listening to us? We're nobody."

I smile. "You're a famous *CelebVid* star."

"Former *CelebVid* star. Now I'm a plucky independent correspondent." Her chin lifts a fraction, but her expression remains blank.

"We're foreigners in a nation governed by a repressive regime. It's safe to assume everything is being recorded. The only secure communications are via audio-implant, and then only if it's point-to-point. Short range. Anything routed through their system, even if it's encrypted, isn't safe."

Elodie ducks her head, but I can see the smirk she's hiding. "I know. I paid attention during your briefing on the ship. But I'm still nobody."

"You're probably right." Her head pops up in surprise, and I suppress a smirk of my own. "But you are an opportunity for good publicity. As long as you don't film anything they want to keep hidden, you're probably fine. I'm sure they'll assign someone to keep you out of trouble."

Her shoulders go back. "I don't need a nanny."

I don't bother responding—if they choose to assign a guide, we won't have a choice.

Arun returns followed by a small army. Four of them wear heavy coveralls with gloves and hats. They carry tool kits, and one has a long, flexible thing draped around his shoulders like a snake—the replacement gasket. The workers climb the shuttle's ramp, gathering by the rear hatch. Three others—two women and a man dressed in Commonwealth business attire—stay with Arun as he joins Dima. Elodie and I move closer.

"Elodie, Va—Lindsay, these are your guides, Naunet and Risa.

They'll show you around Petrograd while I complete my business." Arun gestures to the two women.

The shorter one—a brunette with a sleek updo and small diamond studs in her ears—steps forward. "Naunet Kladinskova at your service." She bumps her knuckles against mine in a way that feels natural. Her voice is clear but faintly accented, and my system tells me she's speaking Standard not being overridden by the translator. She must have spent some time in the Commonwealth to be this fluent. "This is my colleague, Risa van Khumalo."

Risa is tall and broad. A short fringe of blonde hair protrudes from a cylindrical, furry hat that looks out of place with her fitted jacket and pencil skirt. "It is pleasant to meet you." Her voice is deep and heavily accented. She hesitantly offers her fist, and Elodie and I tap ours against it.

"Which nanny do you want?" I ask Elodie through the audio call. She wisely ignores me.

Another wheeled vehicle—this one long, sleek, and dark—rolls to a stop. Risa pulls a handle at the mid-point of the rectangular body. A door hinges up and a two-step ladder drops down. She sweeps a hand at them. "We have the *limuzin* for you—very comfortable. After you, please."

Elodie inclines her head and climbs the short ladder, disappearing into the large vehicle. I follow. Inside, two long, padded bench seats face each other across a narrow aisle. The ceiling and upper half of the walls are transparent, although they appeared opaque from the outside. I take a seat near the back, angling my legs so my knees don't hit Elodie's. I don't like being this far from the exit, but I'm confident I can escape and take Elodie with me if necessary.

Risa joins us, sitting beside Elodie. Naunet pokes her head through the open door. "All set? Good. The seat restraints are automatic. Lift your hands, please."

In response to Elodie's wide-eyed look, I nod, then lift my hands from my thighs, holding them away from my body. A strap about four centimeters wide snakes out of the gap between the seat and the backrest and slides across my lap, disappearing into the slot on the other side. Another strap slips over my shoulder and diagonally across my body to disappear into the same place.

"The shoulder belt will allow movement, but lock in the case of an abrupt stop. The lap belt stays snug at all times." Naunet gives Risa a nod. "I will ride with the driver, to direct him. I'll see you when we reach the Hall of Heroes." She backs away, and the door hinges down to close with a thud.

All external sound is cut off. I check my audio implant—Elodie's link is still active, but I can't reach Arun. They have good shielding on this boat. I turn to Risa. "What is the Hall of Heroes?"

She clears her throat. "I apologize. My *yazyk sodruzhestvo* is not fluent." My translator overrides the Gagarian words: Commonwealth Standard.

I raise an eyebrow at Elodie and trigger the audio link. "They put the one who can't speak Standard back here to get us to speak freely in front of her."

"We ain't that big o' rubes." I'm not sure what she's quoting… if she is. But she clearly understands the situation.

The vehicle's sound proofing may be excellent, but the ride leaves something to be desired. The big tires rumble over a road that looks smooth but isn't. The seat vibrates unevenly under my rear end, and the floorboards bounce beneath my feet.

As we travel between warehouses and more ship repair shops, Risa lumbers through a memorized speech about the great explorers who colonized Gagarin many centuries ago. The Hall of Heroes memorializes these founding fathers with displays about their lives and discoveries. After a few stilted paragraphs, she taps a control panel at the front of the vehicle which blacks out the windows.

"Hey!" Elodie's gaze jerks from the now opaque plasglass to Risa. "I'd like to see the city."

Risa frowns and waves at the screen between us and the driver that is now a two-dimensional display showing the Great Seal of the Gagarian Union—a scrawny scavenger animal with large teeth surrounded by a circle of prickly-looking green leaves. "This are important informations about the heroes. This part of city is not interesting."

Music swells, and the seal fades. Colorful images flash across the screen, depicting ancient spaceships and their rustic equipment. A voice-over begins, describing the same heroes Risa mentioned, but in much greater detail.

"I wonder what they don't want us to see?" Elodie's voice comes through my implant.

"Good question. We flew over the city when we landed. Whatever they're hiding must be only visible from street level."

"Actually, we didn't fly over this part of the city. The Gagarians have a strict air traffic flow that took us *around* Petrograd. I thought it was a noise reduction thing, but maybe there's something else."

"Good catch." I let my gaze drift away from the display, but nothing is visible outside the vehicle. Risa catches my eyes and jerks her head at the screen like a teacher insisting her students pay better attention. I suppress an eye roll and focus on the boring vid.

If there are parts of this city they don't want us to see, then sneaking away from Elodie and our handlers might be harder than I anticipated. I still need to do my data pickup at Eliana's Bakery. According to my map, it's only a few blocks from the Hall of Heroes. I was hoping I could give my escorts the slip while they toured the memorial. But if they're trying to hide something, they'll keep us on a short leash.

"What's out there?" I ask Risa.

She frowns, then pauses the vid. "The city."

I give her a "no, duh," look. "But what part of the city? Residential? Industrial? Slums?"

Her nose goes up. "Gagarin has no slums. This is worker housing. There is nothing of interest."

Elodie leans forward, her seat belt bringing her up short. "But that's exactly what I—and my viewers—want to see! Regular life on Gagarin. It's why we wanted to go to Korsov's Deli! Where the workers eat!"

Risa nods. "You will see Korsov's Deli. Your *rodonachal'nik* requested it." The translator substitutes *patriarch*.

"Our patriarch?" Elodie asks. "Who do you mean?"

Risa's eyes narrow, and she examines Elodie's face—probably looking for a translating device. "Your patron, Mister Kinduja. He is the head of your family, no?"

"Our family? Noooo—" Elodie draws the word out. "He's the captain of our spacecraft, so I suppose that—"

"Yes, your *kapitan*. He asks that we take you to Korsov's; we go to Korsov's. But first, we see the Hall of Heroes." She nods decisively and turns the video back on.

SIX

The Hall of Heroes is as boring as I expected. It's also wildly apocryphal, at least according to the Commonwealth's standard history curriculum. I haven't studied Gagarin in detail, but the briefing I got from the CCIA before taking this mission matched my memories of fifth grade history class pretty closely. That briefing also mentioned the GU's habit of rewriting history to put themselves in the best possible light.

I'm skeptical enough to think the Commonwealth has probably done the same. As they say, history is written by the victors.

But the Heroes of Gagarin must have been super heroic saints and military geniuses. They built a society on the largely inhospitable planet left to them by the greedy Commonwealth, turning bitter survival into a triumphant paradise of human engineering. At least, that's how my app translates the placards. The fact that the Commonwealth didn't exist when humans left Earth doesn't seem to matter. Risa and Naunet give a carefully sanitized version of this story, obviously written to keep from offending wealthy Commonwealth investors. It's also much closer to the narrative I remember from fifth grade.

"The ships were assigned to the five habitable planets and colonists were assigned to ships based on their skills, to ensure an equitable distribution of engineers, doctors, and agriculturalists. Universities contributed top scholars and data scientists to each planet, to ensure the knowledge gained over millennia on Earth would be preserved…"

I tune Naunet out, trying to appear interested while I scope out the building. Elodie doesn't bother being polite. She launches one of her vid drones and flies it through the structure, filming the glowing windows and spectacular architecture. It zooms above the heads of the twenty other tourists wandering through the venue. Twenty tourists who wear suspiciously uniform clothing and show a complete disinterest in the foreign visitors. Plants, obviously.

The Hall of Heroes is a huge cathedral-like structure. Thick stone columns support a vaulted ceiling, and colorful windows glow with scenes from Gagarin's history. The sides of the structure are open to the gardens surrounding the place, and the cold wind bites my face and hands. I crank up the temperature on my heated clothing, hoping Elodie wore the gear I recommended.

Despite the frigid weather, neither of our guides wears a coat or wrap. Risa's furry hat seems to keep her warm—or maybe she has heated undergarments. Naunet keeps her hands in her tunic pockets, but her eyes water and her ears, visible under her elegant updo, are red.

As Naunet narrates, Risa points out the images and statues of the various heroes, each depicted as handsome, strong, and manly. Time to cause some commotion. I lift a hand and interrupt the monologue. "Where are the women?"

Naunet blinks at me. Risa mutters something which my translator doesn't catch. She nods briskly and turns back to me. "No women."

"What do you mean?" Elodie's attention snaps back to the women. "There had to be women. Y'all didn't spring from your founding fathers' heads, fully armed."

That sounds like another quote. I need to get a study guide to Elodie-speak.

Naunet grits her teeth—is it anger at our questions or to keep her teeth from chattering? "Of course there were female colonists. They supported their patriarchs, bore their children, made their homes comfortable."

"Barefoot and pregnant," Elodie grumbles through the audio implant. Aloud, she says, "Really? None of the women did anything heroic?"

Risa draws herself up to her full intimidating height, her Standard becoming more broken as the emotion wells up. Her breath condenses in the glacial air, forming clouds and dissipating. "Every things they did is heroic. Only *surviving* on this planet needs heroic in colonial years. But women is not leaders, is not heroes. Women is providing support and help to their—"

"Yeah, yeah, supporting the patriarch." Elodie rolls her eyes and turns away in disgust. "When did you finally achieve equality?"

The two Gagarians exchange a look but don't answer.

Elodie looks over her shoulder and raises a brow. "That's what I thought."

"Hush!" I hiss through our audio link. "You want to get thrown in the *gulag*?"

"Isn't that an ancient search engine?" When I start to correct her, she cuts me off. "I know it's a prison. But this kind of sexism just— wow. I've heard of it but never really experienced it myself."

"Lucky you."

She whips around, but I give her a warning look. "We'll talk about it later. For now, keep your cool, okay?" Having Elodie whip up some trouble so I can sneak away seemed like a good plan, but I don't want to get her arrested or expelled from the planet.

Risa gives Naunet a significant look, then wanders away to the far corner of the structure. Probably reporting our reactions to her supervisors. Naunet tries to draw our attention to another of the statues, but after a few aborted attempts to engage us, she gives up. "Perhaps it is time to move on to the next destination?"

"Korsov's Deli, right?" Elodie retrieves her drone and stows it in her pocket. "I'm hungry."

As unintended punctuation, her stomach rumbles loudly. I bite back a chuckle.

"Korsov's Deli," Risa confirms. She checks her bulky wrist device, which seems to serve the same function as a holo-ring, although far less elegantly. "It is almost time. I will call the car."

"According to my mapping app, it's only a few blocks." Elodie flicks her holo-ring, and a map appears in her hand. She stretches it and points. "Why don't we walk? I could get some good footage of the city."

"There is little to see in this neighborhood." Naunet tries to herd us toward the VIP entrance and our waiting vehicle.

Elodie gives her a wide-eyed look. "Little to see? This is the heart of old Petrograd! There's city hall, the Volkov Museum, the Abdullayeva Theater, the Yusupova Library—"

"Unfortunately, these venues are all closed today." Naunet puts a hand on Elodie's back and pushes her forward.

Elodie plants her feet, pointing through the opening between two columns. "I can see people going into the Abdullayeva! We don't need to go in if there's no time, but I'd like to at least walk by and see the outside!"

I follow the direction of her finger to a large, ornately decorated building with a pink exterior and gold trim. It sits like an over-decorated and slightly melted wedding cake between two blocky, blank-faced structures. People stream up and down the steps. Several orderly lines snake across the large plaza in front, moving much faster than the queues at Super Annoying Funland. A kiosk near the entrance seems to be selling tickets or monitoring entries.

"You can send your drone to film." Naunet's teeth rattle as she speaks. "We will monitor from inside the vehicle. I'm sorry I didn't dress for the occasion, but I need to get inside. I thought it would be warmer." She smiles apologetically, teeth visibly chattering.

What kind of tour guide doesn't dress for the weather? I'd bet my best stiletto knife that Naunet "forgot" her coat so she'd have an excuse to keep us inside.

But if they're allowing Elodie to film, maybe they aren't trying to hide the city from us. They might be hiding *us* from the locals. According to intelligence, the average Gagarian lives a much simpler lifestyle than most Commonwealth citizens. Seeing rich visitors from outside their system could provoke unrest. Or trigger attacks on those visitors. The Gagarians wouldn't say that—no authoritarian government wants to admit it can't control its people.

Or maybe they don't want us talking to the locals. I try to remember—do they know we have translators? Naunet and Risa have spoken only Standard to us. We used our translators with Dima, but the women weren't with us at that point. They must know the tech exists. It would be wise to assume anyone wealthy enough to travel here would have it.

Time to poke the bear. I take Elodie's arm and pull her away from our nanny. "Go and get warm. Elodie and I can walk over alone. You can monitor us from the vehicle."

"No. I am your guide. I can't—"

Elodie chimes in. her tone sympathetic. "Really, we insist. I can't believe your company doesn't provide you with appropriate clothing."

This seems to bother Naunet. "I am fully equipped for my job." She flushes, as if the admission—the lie?—bothers her. "I simply misjudged the weather."

Elodie nods as if this makes perfect sense. "I'm sure you often get warm days in the winter. And I get it—your job is to guide us. But there's no need for you to suffer. You can follow us in the vehicle, and we won't tell anyone we walked instead of riding."

"But someone might see—" She clamps her jaw shut. "No, we should all ride."

Is she worried about doing her job properly? Or about being caught not doing it properly? I smirk internally as I stop Elodie from exiting the structure. "Let's go with Naunet. I don't want her to get into trouble. But maybe we can stop for a second in front of the Abdullayeva? Just long enough to get pictures?" I smile hopefully at the guide.

Her shoulders drop in relief. "We can arrange this." She steps between us, putting a hand on each of our backs, and steers us toward the VIP exit.

We walk back to the parking area, where high walls shield us from the pedestrians and other visitors to the Hall of Heroes. The *limuzin* waits, Risa by the open door. Warm air blows out, ruffling the fur of Risa's hat. Naunet hurries to the driver's compartment without waiting to see us inside. Risa makes a curt gesture toward the door.

We climb in and settle into our seats. The *limuzin* snakes through the maze of tall, opaque fence, heading away from the Abdullayeva. Just as Elodie opens her mouth to complain, the vehicle reaches the road and turns to drive around the Hall of Heroes. It's stunning from the outside—a sight we missed on the way in since Risa blanked the windows. This time, we gawk at the soaring roofline with its clean lines and stark white stone. The vehicle's transparent roof gives us the opportunity to enjoy the sight in comfort. If I wasn't anxious to test the boundaries, I'd be quite happy to stay inside and avoid the biting wind.

And if I didn't have a mission to complete.

I memorized a map of the city before we landed, so I know we're only a few blocks to Eliana's Bakery. If we can convince Naunet to let us walk to Korsov's Deli, I can slip away and complete my mission. But how can we convince her? I hate to make a break for it, since I don't want to draw attention, but I will if necessary.

The *limuzin* stops in front of the Abdullayeva, and we stare up at the hideous jumble of stone and plastek. It defies the local stark esthetic, with ruffles, flowers, random knobs, strange fluting, and a section that looks like it's covered in cobwebs. Now that we're closer, we can see the individual tiles that make up the smoother portions—each at least a meter square and each a slightly different shade of pink, giving the structure a mottled appearance.

Elodie flicks her holo-ring. "Can I launch my drone, please? This building is fantastic!"

Risa lifts her wrist device to her lips and mutters something. After a moment, she nods. "I open the window." She presses a button on a small panel near her seat, and the plasglas in the upper half of the door slides down. Cold air seeps in. Risa flips another switch, and the hum of a fan I hadn't noticed before kicks up a notch. The frigid breeze slows to a cold trickle.

Elodie pulls a drone from her pocket and sets it on her knee. A few swipes to her holo-display launches the thing, the low hum louder than usual within the confines of the *limuzin*. It lifts off her lap and buzzes out the window.

Risa presses a button again, and the window closes.

"Oh! I've lost control of the drone!" Elodie swipes through her interface, flinging screens up then away at an increasing rate. "Something is interfering. I need to get outside." She scoots across the aisle and manages to open the door.

I gape for a brief second, then follow her outside, twisting away from Risa's grasping hand. My feet hit the plascrete, and I stumble over a curb separating the vehicle from the pedestrian plaza in front of the theater. A few of the people making their way to the vast flight of steps gaze at us, then turn away.

I jog across the large, open square, darting through two lines of people and skidding to a stop beside my boss. "Nice work, Elodie! How'd you get the door open?"

She looks up from her holo-screen, brow furrowed. "I watched her operate it. It's a manual system. You just flip the button up and pull the handle. Easy." In her palm, the view from the drone's cam swoops up the front of the building, then turns to face the plaza. People dressed in dark, heavy clothing stream across it in orderly lines. Near the middle, two figures stand alone—us. Beside me, Elodie waves, and in her other hand, the gold-clad figure does the same. "We kinda stand out, don't we?"

I look at the view, then around us again. "You do. I blend in." I gesture to my usual form-fitting black.

She snickers. "Yeah, right. Just because you're wearing black doesn't make you look like that." She stretches the image, zooming in on a large woman in a voluminous black coat. A huge fur hat like Risa's covers her head. Heavy boots clomp on the plascrete.

I glance down at my sleek clothing and finger a strand of my copper hair. She's right—I don't blend in here.

"Oops, here comes Naunet." Elodie points at her display. The brunette hurries across the plaza toward us, plowing through a line of people who rush out of her way, then flow back into line behind her.

I jerk my head to the left. "Let's start walking to Korsov's. She can't drag us back into the *limuzin*."

"She can't, but Risa could, and she's right behind Naunet." Elodie points at the vid as we angle away from our pursuers. "Do you think she'd do that in front of all these witnesses?"

"Do you know anyone from Gagarin?"

She frowns but shakes her head. "What difference does that make?"

"It doesn't. But if you did, you'd know they don't care about bad publicity. The GIDK grab people off the streets on the regular. These people wouldn't even blink if Risa drugged us and dragged us back to the *limuzin* by our ankles. But keep filming and keep us in view. Does this thing auto-upload to the ship?"

She nods. "Not constantly—the station isn't in geosynchronous orbit. But whenever it's within line of sight." She slows to flick an icon on her screen. "Looks like we're in luck right now, but we'll lose it in about ten minutes."

I grab her arm, dragging to a stop. "Let's hope it's enough." Swinging her around, I start us on a direct intercept for Naunet and Risa.

"I thought we were avoiding them?"

"We were. We aren't now." I wave at our pursuers as they break through the last line of waiting Gagarians. "There you are! Look at the vids Elodie is getting! They're amazing." I grab Elodie's wrist and shove the holo-screen in front of our nannies' faces. Elodie stumbles, trying to maintain her balance. "Our friends on the ship are really enjoying the chance to see Petrograd. Look, it's us!" I point at the vid.

Naunet frowns. "You are transmitting live?"

"Only to the ship. They'll hold the vid so Elodie doesn't run out of storage. Wave to the crew!" I wave wildly at the sky, and tiny me on the vid follows suit.

Naunet looks doubtfully at the vid, then does a half-hearted finger wave at the drone. Risa does the same, more enthusiastically.

"As long as we're halfway there, how about we finish the walk to Korsov's?" Elodie swings the drone around and indicates a building in the vid. "It's right there. We promise not to cause any problems." She winks at Naunet.

The smaller woman frowns. Risa turns her back to us, then mutters into her wrist device. After a brief pause, she speaks again, then turns back to us, her face sour. She gives Naunet a single, jerky nod.

Naunet sweeps a hand in the direction we had been going. "Please, after you."

Elodie falls into step beside the smaller Gagarian while Risa and I bring up the rear. As we progress across the plaza, people scurry out of our way, then close in behind us. We're like a spoon through pudding, except we never get close enough to speak to any of these people.

Not that pudding speaks. I need to work on my analogies. Maybe later when I'm back on the ship.

With step one accomplished—escaping the vehicle—I need to work on step two. The attentive Risa will make slipping away much more difficult. I sort through my favorite gambits and choose a couple.

A low groan gets me a sideways look from Risa, but no response. I try again, surreptitiously clutching my hand to my gut.

"Are you unwell?" Risa's gaze flicks over me, evaluating.

"It's nothing. Just a little—" I break off with another faint groan. I don't want to overdo it and get sent to a hospital.

"Travel is hard on the digestion."

I frown at Risa. "You've traveled? Have you been to the Commonwealth?"

Her lip curls a little. "No. Lewei. Luna City. Tereshkova once. I have no interest in the Commonwealth." The last word comes out like a curse.

"I feel that way myself sometimes." I try to smile, then swallow hard as if it's too much. "I might need a—" I clutch my stomach again.

"You want a toilet?" She looks around, then yells something to Naunet. My translator says, "This weak foreigner needs a toilet."

Around us, several heads turn in my direction, then quickly look away. The empty gap around us grows as people move a few more centimeters away. I hide a smirk and groan again.

"We will hurry." Risa grabs my arm and increases her speed. With her long legs, I have to run to keep up, which interferes with my acting.

"No, I won't make it!" I rip my arm from Risa's grip and dart toward the nearest storefront.

SEVEN

RISA OVERTAKES me and grips my arm again. "This store is not having public toilet. Next one." She pulls me toward a coffee shop down the street. Shoving the door open, she pushes me into the warm space. Dark-clothed patrons look up from the industrial tables, then hurriedly look away. I make a mental note to look up the logo on Risa's collar. Based on reactions so far, I'd guess the local populace knows this tour company is a front for the GIDK. Risa shouts another embarrassing explanation at the startled woman behind the counter, then pushes me through a door at the rear of the building.

We stop in a short hallway. A swinging door with a round window on the right leads to the kitchen. On the left, there are two doors with the universal sign for sanitation facilities as well as the word "toilet" in Standard. I hurry past the first one and duck into the second, still holding my belly.

The small room contains a toilet and a sink. A high window lets in the frigid breeze. I lock the door and flick through my holo-ring apps, then let out a few louder groans. My system records the sounds, and I run those through a modifier. Pulling a tiny speaker from my internal jacket pocket, I swipe the recording to it and set it to replay at irregular intervals with random variations.

The window is too small to escape through, but I don't need to leave the building. According to my memorized map, Eliana's bakery is only two streets away. I pull one of the utilitarian clips from my hair and detach the tiny CCIA drone hidden beneath it. It's less than a centimeter in length and actually looks like an insect if you don't inspect it too carefully. A trained operative would undoubtedly recognize it, which is why it stays hidden in my hair. If any Gagarian gets that close to my head, I'm in bigger trouble. Or, rather, they are.

I activate the data transmission protocol and use my personal codes to authorize it. Pausing to turn on the sink, I fly the device out the window. The faint buzz should be inaudible through the door, but the running water provides additional cover.

Someone knocks on the door, and I jump. Risa's voice comes clearly through the thin door. "Are you needing medical attention?"

"No—ooooh!" The automated groan interrupts my reply. When it ends, I go on. "I think I ate something on the ship—Just a few more minutes and I'll be fi—ahhhh."

A grunt is the only response. Which is fine with me—I have work to do. Using my holo-ring, I guide the drone over the tops of the low buildings, heading directly toward the bakery.

Another agent—a deep plant here in Petrograd—has hidden a connection node in the bakery. That device passively monitors electronic traffic within twenty meters and will switch to send and receive mode if it detects a CCIA signal. Then the data transmission happens automatically.

Normally, these are set so an agent can stroll through the building and trigger the drop. But the bakery is in a single-story building, so flying low enough should trigger the transfer. I lower the drone to a half-meter above the flat roof, then hit the ping button.

The node responds almost immediately, and the data transfer begins. The little meter on my holo-screen starts to fill from the left, the percentage counting down as the data is transmitted. I take the few seconds of down-time to use the facilities—never pass up food, sleep, or a bathroom is my motto. As the screen flicks from eighty-five to ninety percent, I flush. "I'll be out in a minute!"

Another grunt comes through the door. That thing must be made of paper—it sounds like Risa is in the room with me. I flick off my audio and restore the speaker to my jacket pocket. As I push my hands into water still flowing into the sink, my holo-ring flashes red.

"Zark!"

"What? You need doctor?"

"No!" I look around the room, but there's nothing to blame. With a grimace, I splash some water down my pantleg. "The sink got me." Shaking water from my hands, I swipe frantically through the screens. My data transfer seems to have alerted a warning system—red alerts flash across my palm. I scan them as I swipe them away. The first two might be the bakery's net connection noticing illicit activity, but the others imply the bakery's system might have alerted a government response. I hold my breath as the last two percent of the transmission ticks slowly across the meter.

The second it flashes to "transmission complete," I flick the self-destruct command. The vid goes blank as the device sends a surge of power through its own circuits. These things are designed to save the last bit of juice for an automatic wipe, but since I only flew it a few hundred meters, there should have been sufficient charge to literally melt the internal electronics. If the GIDK search the roof of the bakery, they *might* find the miniscule drone, but it will be impossible to read. And the data is now secure in my holo-storage.

I flick off the system, dry my hands, and open the door with a smile. "I'm feeling—"

There's no one in the hallway.

Out of curiosity, I try the door at the end of the hall. It opens, leading to a narrow, dingy alley. The buildings behind this one loom closer than they appeared in the drone footage. There's no sign of Risa out here, so I head for the coffee shop.

Risa, Naunet, and Elodie sit at the table by the window. They each have a pastry and a steaming beverage in front of them. Risa's eyes flick to me, then away. She says something to Naunet, who looks over her shoulder, then rises. She meets me halfway across the shop, which is now empty except for us. "Would you like some coffee and a pastry?"

"Tea, if they have it. No milk." I pat my stomach. "And no food, thanks. Just to be safe."

Naunet gives me a sympathetic nod, then turns to order from the woman behind the counter. My translator dutifully converts the brief conversation to Standard: tea to go, black, sugar on the side.

I nod my thanks and join the others. "I thought we were going to Korsov's?"

"Oh, we are." Elodie slurps down the last of her coffee and stands, the half-eaten pastry in her hand. "But I couldn't pass up these yummies! Look at the filling in this!" She shoves the flaky turnover at me, and a glob of red filling flies loose, narrowly missing my damp pants.

I take a step back, holding up my hands and making a face. "Please, no food!"

"You're going to hate Korsov's then!" Elodie pulls her pink coat on over her blue and green dress and matching pink leggings. "Let's go!"

I do a double take. "Weren't you wearing gold before?"

"Color-change fabric!" Using an app on her holo-ring, she gleefully demonstrates five or six different color combinations. Naunet, Risa, and the woman behind the counter enthusiastically applaud each one.

"Then why did you need a suitcase full of clothes?" I make a mental note to find out where she bought that outfit. Hidden beneath my sleek black "uniform" lives the heart of a fashionista.

Elodie shakes her head sadly. "This only changes the colors, not the style."

Fair point.

Naunet hands me a recyclable cup as I follow Elodie out the door. I nearly drop the hot container. "Yikes!" I pull my sleeve down over my hand to protect my fingers. I won't be drinking that any time soon.

As we exit the building, a dark-windowed vehicle speeds by, followed by another one. They skid around the corner, headed in the general direction of the bakery. Risa presses her finger to her ear, then moves away to mutter into her bulky wrist device.

My heartrate increases, so I take a few deep breaths to slow it down. I don't know if the Gagarians have vital sign scanners, like the Commonwealth does, or if we've done anything sufficiently suspicious to trigger their use. If I were Risa, I'd have automated scans on a regular schedule with a threshold alert.

I wish I could come up with a reason to take Elodie back to the ship. I could play up the food-poisoning, but she'd just want to come back tomorrow. And she knows I have an iron constitution—I don't need her questioning my motives. Her complete ignorance of my CCIA employment is one of the most important pieces of my cover story.

"What's going on?" Elodie increases her pace toward the corner the vehicles just rocketed around, practically bouncing with excitement. Her drones soar ahead and out of sight.

"Nothing." Naunet, now wearing a heavy coat she must have had in the *limuzin*, grabs Elodie's arm as we reach the street crossing. "Be careful of traffic."

We look at the empty streets. There weren't a lot of vehicles earlier, but there are none now. The pedestrians seem to have melted away, leaving us alone on the sidewalk. The dark transports have disappeared.

Elodie lifts her drone's holo-vid to eye level and stretches it larger so we can all see. A dozen people clothed in black, complete with hoods over their faces, stream out of two dark cars and into a storefront. The sign above the door reads Eliana's Bakery. "What's happening? Isn't that the place you wanted to visit, Vanti?"

Our Gagarian nurserymaids stare at her vid. Elodie smiles at me, oblivious to my death glare. Then I notice a glint in her eyes. Is she really this clueless, or is she messing with me? I give my best non-answer. "I didn't *want* to go there—but it was on your original agenda. I guess it's a good thing you rescheduled."

"Recall your drones." Naunet grabs Elodie's wrist and shakes it. "We must not—you don't want to interfere. In whatever that is." She darts a nervous look at Risa, her tone intense. The other woman has moved a few steps away, where she mutters into her device, her gaze focused beyond us.

"Please, stop recording." Naunet shakes Elodie's hand again. "We can't allow—" She breaks off, her gaze going back to the larger Gagarian.

Elodie flicks a few commands, and the vid changes as the drone glides down the street, away from the activity. When the screen goes blank, Elodie cries out. "What happened? My drone isn't responding!"

"The GIDK probably used a local signal crusher." I watch Risa as I speak, but she's focused on her conversation and doesn't react. "They can draw a virtual curtain around a location and deactivate any electronics in the area. That drone is probably toast."

"You mean dead? Or just shut down?" Elodie swipes through diagnostics. "I'm getting nothing—it's not connecting at all. Even with the ship." She glances up, as if she can see the *Ostelah Veesta* in orbit above us. "No, wait, the ship is over the horizon." She pulls away from Naunet's grip. "I need to go get my drone."

"No!" Naunet and I yell in unison.

Across the way, Risa's head snaps around, like a laser sight locking on target. "What is problem?"

"Nothing." I put a hand on Elodie's arm and give her another death glare. "No problem at all."

"But—"

"We don't need to get your drone back, Elodie." I squeeze her forearm in warning. "You can get a new one. It's not worth upsetting the local authorities. They obviously didn't want you filming."

Elodie rounds on Risa. "Next time we're in an area where filming is not permitted, I'd appreciate a heads up. I was recalling it. Those things are not free!"

"Perhaps today's tour should be suspended," Naunet suggests. "You can go back to your ship and get a new drone. And we can visit Korsov's tomorrow."

Elodie gives the woman a once-over, then looks at Risa. Something in the taller woman's face or body language gets through to her. She nods regally. "I don't know what happened here—" She waves both hands in the general direction of the bakery. "I don't really care. But I do care that you destroyed my property. Maybe I won't bother coming back tomorrow."

"We will contact you with a new itinerary for tomorrow." Naunet watches Risa as she says this, as if seeking approval. "For now, I'm recalling the *limuzin*."

We pile into the vehicle when it arrives, and the windows go dark. "For your protections," Risa says. "There is possible terrorist activity in this area. That is problem—for why drone is disable. Police must download your video." She taps her ear. "Government will return device if possible."

"If possible? You mean they might have destroyed it? Or are they taking it apart and stealing my footage?" Elodie's voice ratchets higher.

I give up on the death glares. They aren't working on Elodie. Instead, I put a hand on her arm. "They didn't 'steal' your drone. Remember, Gagarian laws are different from the Commonwealth. They are within their rights to use civilian footage in an investigation. And they aren't required to ask permission."

Elodie splutters for a few minutes, then goes silent.

"Can we change the window setting so we can see out?" I tap the glass. "I'm sure Gagarin has one-way windows?" I put a little doubt into that statement. Nothing like a good passive-aggressive jab to provoke patriotic pride.

Risa crosses her arms and stares me down. "This *limuzin* is not equipped with that ability."

So much for that idea. Obviously she was told to keep us in the dark. "I guess we don't rate the good stuff."

"I'll let Helva know we're coming back early." Elodie flicks her holo-ring and swipes through a few screens.

"Who is Helva?" Risa asks, idly.

Zark. We can't let the Gagarin government know we have an AI shuttle, and I'm ninety-nine percent sure Risa is GIDK. "She's part of the crew. Up on the ship. Elodie just wants to let her know we'll come back early—in case she's on the station." I've spent a lot of years perfecting my ability to lie my way out of sticky situations. Why does Risa make me nervous? I'm practically babbling!

"Good save!" Elodie says over the audio as she stares at her holo-screen.

"Was that sarcasm?"

She looks up, surprise on her face. "No. I'm serious. That was completely believable." She turns to Risa and speaks aloud. "All set. They'll be ready for us to dock."

The *limuzin* rolls to a stop, and the windows clear. We're in front of Bondarenko and Sons. "You don't need to wait for your captain?" Risa opens the door. "Or for the repairs to be completed?"

I follow Risa and check for threats, but I suspect the GIDK has already cleared this location. There are no other customers.

"They finished the door seal an hour ago." Elodie climbs out. "Arun forwarded their message to me."

A little twinge of jealousy sparks through me. Why did Arun contact Elodie instead of me? The voice of reason tells me to get my emotions under control. That Elodie is his passenger, and I'm just part of the entourage. Jealous Vanti tells reasonable Vanti to shut up. "They may not release the ship to you, since you aren't the owner." And she's a woman, but I don't bother saying that. It would just upset Elodie again for no reason.

She shakes her head as she strikes out across the plasphalt toward the gate on the side of the building. "Arun has already settled the bill. And I have an unlock code for the gate, so we're good. We can wait in the shuttle." She stops by the gate through the tall force fence surrounding the landing pad. When we arrived, the *limuzin* drove out to the ship, but I guess without Arun, we aren't worth the trouble. Or Naunet and Risa are anxious to get away.

"Thanks for the tour, ladies." Elodie bumps fists with the two guides. "A shame it was cut short. And please let me know when and how I can get my drone back."

Risa presses her ear and speaks into her wrist. After a moment, she nods and looks up. "I am sorry. The drone is unavailable. We will see you tomorrow."

Naunet grimaces. "Sometimes the signal crusher damages electronics in close proximity. It may have fried your drone."

Or the drone was confiscated. "Thanks for your help." I press a hand against my stomach. "I hope to feel better tomorrow."

Elodie sends a signal to the force fence, and the gate dissolves, leaving a human-sized door in the field. With a negligent wave, she steps through, and I follow. Another command from Elodie's ring, and the fence reforms behind us.

A creeping feeling skitters down my spine—the force shield is no protection from the GIDK, if they take an interest in us. Time to get off the planet.

EIGHT

Arun strides down the shuttle's rear ramp. His hair is uncharacteristically messy, and he looks distracted. "I was just going to recall you. We need to go. Gear up in ten. I've started the launch checklist." He jerks his head at the front of the ship, and Elodie scurries past him.

"What's happened?" I follow her up the ramp, Arun at my side, his hand pressed against my lower back.

He shakes his head but doesn't reply. Something so sensitive he doesn't want to discuss it on Gagarin soil? I could activate a voice call, but the fact that he didn't do that makes me think he doesn't trust the tech to be secure.

Is it? I've always been told a point-to-point call at this distance—we're physically touching—is as safe as a whispered conversation in a faraday cage vault, but maybe the Gagarians have something we don't know about.

The idea is chilling. Most Gagarian tech is based on stolen Commonwealth gear. Purchased and illegally reverse engineered, leaked specs, poached technicians—they've used every trick in the book for centuries to keep up with us. But what if that's partially a front? What if they've secretly been developing their own tech which they've kept hidden from us?

I shake my head as I take my seat and fasten my restraints. We've got our own spies. If they've cracked the private audio call, we'll know.

Curled in the empty seat, Apawllo opens one eye and yawns. It feels like an eye roll. Great, now even the cat knows more than I do. Or thinks he does.

"Checklist complete." Elodie swipes through a few screens. "We're green to launch."

"Control says we're cleared to go." Arun swipes his own holograms this way and that. "Runway two-five. Have you done a horizontal launch before?"

Elodie shakes her head. "Why would I? What's the point?"

He gestures. "They've got older aircraft here that aren't capable of vertical takeoff. And they like to keep a tight control on where we travel. You might have noticed we skirted around the city on our descent. They claim it's a noise issue, but…" His nose wrinkles as he drives the shuttle toward the runway. "Horizontal launch means they can send us exactly where they want us to go. If we just lift off, we can go where we want." His hand rises in illustration, banking left and right. "I suppose we could anyway, but if we want to come back, we need to follow the rules."

The ship slows as he turns it to face the runway, then we rocket forward. The artificial gravity compensates for the speed, so there's no g-force pressing us back into our seats. The effect is like watching a two-dimensional video.

We lift off the ground and follow the green lines projected on the front windows, soaring up and away from Petrograd. Within a few minutes, we reach low orbit.

"I'm running a scan for—" Arun glances back at me. An icon flashes red, and he turns to read it, then looks at me again. "You wanna…?"

I unfasten my restraints and stand. He flicks a program slip at me, and my holo-ring vibrates in response. "Got it."

"What—"

He holds up a hand, cutting off Elodie's question. "Two more."

My ring vibrates again, and I flash a thumbs up as I head to the rear of the ship.

The haptics take me straight to the first bug. Like most Gagarian tech, they're larger than their Commonwealth counterparts. I take the pea-sized seed and drop it into an isolation envelope, then look for the next two. Another vibration indicates a fourth one.

When I've gotten them all, I scan with my own tech and find two smaller ones. These are the size of a poppy seed, unnoticeable without a scan. They look remarkably like the chip on the tiny drone I sent to the bakery earlier today.

"I found two more." I lift the sealed envelope as I return to the front. "Smaller. Looks like Commonwealth tech, not copies."

Elodie's head turns, and she gives me a quick look. "How do you know?"

"I have a more powerful scanner. Something I got when I was still working for SK2." That's true, but I didn't get the tech *from* SK2.

"No, I mean how do you know what Commonwealth tech looks like? I assume you aren't talking about stuff that's available for sale." Her blue eyes sparkle and her lips twitch.

I keep forgetting Elodie is smarter than she lets on. I need to stop underestimating her. "I'm a security specialist, so part of my job is knowing what's out there. Several of these devices were as small as anything I've seen in the field. If you remember, everything on Gagarin was kind of clunky. Did you see those wrist things?" I twist my holo-ring on my finger, illustrating the difference.

"Is it safe to talk, then?" Helva asks.

I cover my eyes. "If it isn't, we're in trouble now."

Helva laughs. "Just because I was hiding while we were on the planet doesn't mean I wasn't watching. I saw every device they planted. And you and Arun got them all."

"Thanks, Helva. That's reassuring." Arun pats the dashboard, then rotates his seat so he's facing halfway between me and Elodie in front of me. "We have a problem."

Apawllo stretches, then leaps to the back of my seat, lying across the top of the headrest as if he wants to join the conversation.

Arun tracks the cat's progress, then returns his gaze to me. "They've got Leo."

Elodie gasps. Apawllo yawns.

"Who does?" I swipe open my link to the *Ostelah* and pull security footage.

Arun lifts both hands. "I only know what Raynaud told me. Someone broke through security protocols and grabbed Leo. He wasn't on the ship—he was in the corridor."

I slap a hand over my eyes again. "I told him to stay aboard."

In the commercial section of the station, a rented berth included a private corridor from your airlock to the public areas of the station. But the security on the hatch to the station is controlled by the station, not us. I have little faith in security I don't control.

"I'm sure he thought he'd be safe there." Elodie taps her fingers on the dash. "I mean, they let us set our own secure passcodes."

Arun nods. "Sure, but the station has overrides. And if the government was behind this, getting the station to use those overrides would be nothing. The only completely safe space is inside the ship."

"Even that…" I let the statement die. "I knew letting him come with us was a risk, but I didn't think they'd grab him so fast. How'd they know he was here? And that he was in the corridor?"

"Cams." Helva's voice has a "duh" quality to it. "They watched until he came out, and they grabbed him. And before you start ranting about his stupidity, they could have engineered an emergency that would require an evacuation."

"I don't rant. But good point." I hate agreeing with the computer. No, that's not true. I hate that the computer thought of it before I did.

Computers don't think, Vanti. True artificial intelligence has never been achieved. So-called AIs mimic intelligence, but they aren't capable of completely original thought. Of course, neither are humans. Everything we think has roots in something else. But what we call AIs are not sentient. Helva sure does a good job of faking it though. That sneer was subtle.

"How do we get him back?" Elodie asks.

I flick through a few screens on my ring. "How far out of orbit can you fly, Helva?"

"I'm not capable of interstellar flight because I don't have jump drives. But my range is restricted only by *your* needs. Life support, food, water. Without you softshells, I could fly back to Sally Ride. It would take a while, but I could do it."

Arun chuckles. "A while? At your top speed, it would take a couple of centuries."

"A couple of centuries isn't that long when your programming will last forever."

Great. Now our AI has delusions of immortality. I clear my throat. "I don't need to go to S'Ride. I want to get beyond the Gagarian surveillance systems so I can send a message back to—" I catch Elodie's gaze. A small smirk plays around her lips. "Back to some friends who might help us."

Elodie rolls her eyes. "I know you work for the government, Vanti. Why else would you have agreed to be my security? I don't pay anywhere near what you made at SK2. I checked."

"You know how much I made on SK2?"

"I might have friends who have access to the payroll records." She laughs. "You aren't the only one who can be sneaky. But I don't mind being your cover. That's what you call it, right? The job that you pretend to do so you can do your real job?"

"I don't *pretend* to protect you!"

"Not usually. Until something more important takes priority." Elodie nods as if this makes sense. "You have no idea what I was doing on Tereshkova while you and Arun were snooping around that amusement park."

"I took a day off! Why do you think that was a job? We were just enjoying the—"

"Could we focus, please?" Helva ramps up her volume to drown out our argument. "We have a missing crew member, and we need to get him back. What's his story? Why'd they want him?"

Helva must not have access to our personal records. Which makes sense. Why would Arun have Leo's secret identity in his computer system? He's a passenger, not crew. Although, if we were in the Commonwealth when she came out of training mode, I'm sure she would have done a few searches.

There I go, anthropomorphizing the ship again.

"Leonidas is not his real name." I flip through a few more screens as I talk, trying to multi-task and doing it badly—but better than the average human. "His birth name is Ervin Zhang, and he's the son of the former dictator of Lewei. He left Lewei a decade ago and has been living in the Commonwealth. He usually works as a chef. We thought he'd be safe—or at least mostly safe—in Gagarin."

"Gagarin and Lewei have much stronger ties than either of them have with the Commonwealth." Helva's voice takes on a lecturing tone.

"Yes, we know." I cut her off before she can launch into a full-on dissertation. "I guess we thought his identity was still secret. Or at least, secret enough. But someone obviously knew he was a valuable target, and they arranged to grab him. So, how do we find out who took him? And can we get him back before they sell him to Lewei?"

Elodie raises her hand, as if she's in school. "Why would Lewei want him? He was practically a kid when he left. And his father isn't in power anymore. It's not like anyone could use him for leverage against the current regime."

I rock my hand back and forth. "The current premier is his uncle, I think. But it sounds like they weren't close. It doesn't really matter why they took him. We need to get him back."

"How do we do that?" Arun slumps in his seat.

"The first step is to fly beyond surveillance. I can send a message to —" I glance at Elodie and sigh. "I can send a message to my people and see what they can tell us. But if we have to rescue him, it will be up to us."

Elodie looks at Arun. "Are you willing to risk your reputation? If the government was involved in grabbing him, you could lose access to the markets here."

I stare at Elodie, my jaw slack. She comes off as this fluffy bimbo most of the time, then she contributes something like that.

Arun sits up straight. "Leo was on my ship. No one kidnaps my crew and gets away with it. And if that means I can never trade in Gagarin again, so be it. I don't need the business that badly." He lifts a hand. "Don't get me wrong. I think the new markets in Gagarin are going to make early adopters a load of credits. But I won't trade Leo for that."

Arun might be one of the least "top-lev-ish" top-levs I've ever met.

NINE

WHEN WE PASS THE STATION, Helva checks in with flight control. They warn us we're leaving the Gagarin Service Area, and if we get into trouble, rescue could be delayed. In other words, if something goes wrong with our shuttle and we all die, it's not their fault. I raise a brow at Arun, and he returns a self-satisfied smirk.

When we first boarded the *Ostelah Veesta*, I did a complete review of the ship, of course. I checked all the maintenance records, made sure we had redundancies in life support, and stored some extra emergency rations in my cabin. I ran security checks on the operating systems and even scanned the crew's private data. I didn't read anything personal—I'm not a snoop. But I ran everything through my very thorough software. I checked this shuttle along with the rest of the ship, so I'm confident a short jaunt outside the GSA will be trouble-free.

I'm still disappointed I missed Helva, but I guess that's proof she's good at hiding. Although the song she's currently blasting out into the black might raise some questions.

Helva is an in-system shuttle, so the trip out of the GSA takes a couple of hours. She regales us with a vast library of music ranging from ancient chants to ear-splitting modern p-funk. Arun finally asks her to lower the volume so we can hear our conversation. She complies, but the next seven songs all have themes of disappointment and abandonment.

I grit my teeth. The *Ostelah* could have gotten us here in minutes, but I'm not ready to have Arun undock from the station. There might be intel to be gathered there. Which reminds me…

"Arun, can you get into the station databases? See if you can find out who leaked Leo's identity to the kidnappers? Maybe we can trace it back to them."

Arun nods and flicks his holo-ring with a grin. "I started my spiders remotely the moment Raynaud contacted me. I haven't uncovered anything yet, but it's only a matter of time."

"Perfect. I've got my message written and encrypted. When we reach the safe zone, I'll send it off."

Elodie strokes the cat. "How do you send it? Don't you need to connect to the jump beacon through the station's comm system?"

I smirk. "I have… alternate routes."

Her eyes widen. "Like a secret comm satellite? Do we have those?"

"If I answered that question—"

"You'd have to shoot me. I know."

"I was going to say I'd have the CIRS audit your taxes, but yeah. I can't answer that. But you remember that news report a few months ago about the Commonwealth finding a Gagarin comm transmitter near Grissom?"

She nods.

"Anything they can do, we can do better." I flick a few more files.

"What good is a secret transmitter if you have to fly out of orbit to use it?" Arun asks. "Shouldn't it be safe to transmit from the planet?"

I give him a flat "I can't answer that" look. "Better safe than sorry. And we're already up here." Plus I don't want my semi-official use of the system to draw attention and potentially endanger the agents who might need it in a life-or-death situation.

He nods, as if he understands what I'm not saying. He and I work together almost as seamlessly as my old partner Griz and I did—but Arun and I have only known each other a few weeks. And most of that time, we weren't together. It's comforting and unsettling at the same time.

Elodie climbs out of her seat and passes me on her way to the back. When I don't hear the click of the sanitation module door, I turn to look. She puts Apawllo down in the center of the small cargo space. "Helva, can you turn off the artificial gravity back here? I want to film Apawllo."

I rub my forehead. "Wha—we have more important things to do than create viral vids, Elodie."

"*You* have more important things to do. I'm sitting around doing nothing. These vids are what pay your—well, supplement your paycheck. You don't want your cover going up in smoke because I can't make a living, do you?" When I don't respond, she calls, "Helva?"

"Sure!" Helva makes a few clicking noises—as if she's flipping switches. But the clicks sound like they're being made with her mouth, not actual switches. If she had a mouth.

Arun chuckles at my dumbfounded face. "She's a character, isn't she?" The words come through my audio implant, his warm, deep voice as intimate as a whisper.

"Is she trying to put us at ease? Because it's having the opposite effect. Machine pretending to be human..."

He shrugs. "When I bought the software, they told me she was quirky. I like quirky. And I might have—" He wiggles his fingers.

"You tweaked her code? AIs are crazy complicated. How do you know you didn't tip her over the edge?"

"She's not sentient. She's very good at imitating self-awareness, but she's just a super-fast, super-accurate information sorting and predictive response engine with access to all of humanity's collected data."

"You are not making me feel any better."

"Whachya two talkin' about?" Helva joins the call.

"Hey!" I say aloud. "You're not supposed to butt into a private conversation, Helva!"

"How did you do that?" Arun swipes rapidly through screens. He growls a little, pushing holos aside and twisting data faster than I can keep up.

I flick open my comm system to check my security. A red icon flashes. I'd swear I had audio and haptic alerts on this system. Why are they deactivated? I reset them, then check the seals on the data packet I have ready to send. As far as I can tell, Helva hasn't breached it. That does not reassure me.

"Got it." Arun's voice is back in my ear. "She's out."

"Are you sure?"

"Yeah, it was my fault. I left a link to my system in the—" He rattles off some arcane programmer stuff. I understand more tech-speak than the average person, but Arun is way out of my league. He seems to notice my silence and blank face. "In other words, it wasn't a security breach. It was my fault, and it won't happen again." He says aloud, "Will it, Helva?"

"Will what?" Helva chirps.

"That proves nothing," I say aloud as I flick my security open again. "How did she deactivate my alerts?"

"I would never do that!" Helva's over-the-top indignation reminds me of a character on one of Triana's *Ancient TēVē* vids. Something called a "soap opera."

"She can't have done that." Arun pulls a screen wide enough to cover the front windows and points at a highlighted section. "See. There's no way for Helva to connect to your holo-ring, and your security settings are activated at the local level."

"There's no way that you know of. She's already proven she can hide from Gagarian scans. How do you know she isn't hiding other capabilities? Who did you buy her from, anyway? I am not comfortable with—"

"We're heeeeere!" Helva sings out, her volume making our supposedly private call difficult to hear. "We've reached the coordinates you gave me, Vanti."

"Thank you, Helva." I push myself up from my seat. My feet leave the deck, then I settle in a slow arc. "Did you reduce the gravity everywhere?"

"Sorry. I didn't think you'd mind. Since you were sitting down." The shuttle hums a little tune. "There you are. Back to normal."

"Helva, please wait for instructions before adjusting gravity." Arun twists his seat to face the front window again and rises. "Do you need any help, Vanti?" His question blocks out Helva's muttered reply.

"Nope, I'm good."

I move between the seats and past the sanitation cubicle. When I reach the open cargo area beyond, my leg pushes my left foot to the decking, but there's no gravity in the cargo space. The force of my landing bounces my foot away from the deck. Momentum keeps me moving forward as my right foot pushes off in regular gravity and swings my body through the gravity border. Even though I'm expecting it, it's hard to compensate, and I float toward the ceiling.

Right past the cat who spins lazily in the center of the space. His limbs and tail splay out in weird directions, and his fur stands out as if he's full of static. He opens an eye long enough to give me a dismissive glare, then closes it again.

"Does he like this?"

Elodie hovers in a corner, watching vid on her holo-ring. She looks up at my question and shrugs, which sends her drifting upward. She grabs a handhold and stops her movement. "He seems to. I got some great vid of him bouncing around the hold. And a hilarious one when he bounced through the border and hit the deck." She chuckles. "Good thing cats always land on their feet."

I shove away from the overhead, aiming for the rear. Using a handhold to arrest my movement before I faceplant into the wall, I rotate and tap a button on the panel nearby. A shield slides aside, revealing a small porthole above the rear hatch. Gagarin spins behind us, like a blue-green marble. The station is too small to see.

"Helva, please rotate the shuttle one hundred and eighty degrees."

"You got it, Vanti."

We rotate to the right, and the planet slides out of sight. The window darkens as the sun heels into view. I turn away until we've swung past, then squint out into the darkness.

"There we are. Pointed back the way we came," Helva says.

I check my system. "Two more degrees, then up by six."

"Two degrees on the X-axis and six on the Y. Roger. Aaaaaaaand mark."

Her cheerful tone is starting to grate. I think she's hoping we'll forget she broke into our comms. I briefly considered a spacewalk to send this message, but if Helva means us harm, intercepting this highly encrypted message isn't going to make a bit of difference. She literally holds our lives in her cargo bay.

I shoot the signal that wakes the comm node. My holo-ring pings with the confirmation, and I send the message packet. One more confirmation, and the node goes back to invisible mode. Activating the system only when transmission is necessary helps keep it hidden. The local agents use it primarily for outbound traffic. If the agency needs to contact agents in the field, other means are used.

Unless it's a Dante Alert, which tells agents to "abandon all hope" and go to ground. If the agency ever has to send a Dante, they aren't expecting to use that node again. And although the official mission statement says the CCIA leaves no one behind, in a Dante situation, no one expects to see those agents again. I've only heard of it happening once, and the single survivor doesn't like to talk about it.

"We can go now." I push off the wall, grabbing the cat as I glide past. He grumbles at me but remains relaxed. When I reach the border, I grab a handle and swing my feet down, cradling Apawllo against my body. One weird, stomach-lurching step, and we're back into normal gravity. I deposit the cat in his seat and drop into the one across the aisle.

Elodie skips past me to the front and straps into her own seat. Arun finishes whatever he's working on and closes his holo-screens. "Ready when you are."

"On it." The little shuttle surges smoothly forward, Helva adjusting the artificial gravity to allow the force to push us back in our seats.

"Gravity in the cargo hold is restored. Estimated return time is—what's that?"

"Elvis?" I smirk as I suggest the deity often invoked on *Ancient TēVē* when trying to distract others.

The ship lurches as if we've run into something. Or been grabbed.

"Not quite," Helva says, her tone tense. "Unless Elvis became a pirate."

TEN

I FLIP OPEN my holo-ring and connect to Helva's external cams. "Pirates?"

"Either that or system police." Helva throws vids up on the main viewscreen. "But they don't look very official."

"No, they do not." Arun grabs a vid and pulls it wider.

A ship glints in the sunlight against a field of stars and black. As he zooms in, details become clear. The ship is a standard gray-white, with old burn marks near its thrusters. "Based on configuration, I'd guess a *fregat* class ship, probably purchased as a military surplus," Helva says. "Scans indicate a photon cannon—not currently active—and a couple of Sorian-class torpedo tubes that appear to be empty."

But it's the red skull and crossbones painted on the front that catches my attention. "They really are pirates." Or pretending to be. My pre-departure briefing on Gagarin indicated the government often contracts with criminal enterprises to carry out their agenda. These "pirates" might haul us back to Gagarin and send us to the gulag. "Open a comm channel."

"Comms are open, but they aren't replying!" Helva mimics the voice of a popular vid star who played a comm tech in a scifi show last year.

What? I watch entertainment vids. Once in a while.

"Keep trying. Let me know if you get through." Arun drums his fingers on his armrest. "Why would they target us? This shuttle isn't big enough to have anything of interest to them."

"Oh, please, we could have a bazillion credits worth of cryptocurrency on board." Elodie grips the dash, her eyes wild as she gazes at the vids. "Or electronics or weapons or—"

"Elodie, you're putting dents in my plastek!" Helva's voice hits like a slap across the face.

Elodie yanks her hands away from the dash.

"I didn't mean we couldn't have *anything* of interest." Arun waves a screen away and pulls up another one. "But it's odd they'd target a random shuttle. We aren't on any schedule. Space is huge. If they just sit out here hoping someone will blunder by, they won't catch anything."

"Except us." I poke at the holo showing the approaching ship. "But you're right. Someone told them we were coming. Just like someone told them about Leo."

"You think it's the same people?" Elodie's gaze pings from me to the vids and back.

"I think it would be an insanely improbable coincidence if they aren't. I got a full briefing on Gagarin before we left the Commonwealth. No reports of random kidnappings or ship seizures. The odds of both hitting us within hours have got to be unbelievably tiny."

"I can calculate that for you," Helva chirps.

"Not necessary." I refrain from rolling my eyes, but I get the distinct feeling she knows.

"But we didn't know we were coming until we came." Elodie bites her lip.

It takes a second to unravel that, then I nod in approval. "Good point. We came out here because of Leo. We would have had no reason to do it if they hadn't grabbed him. But how did they know we'd come? No one knows about that comm node. Certainly not Leo."

Elodie whimpers. "What will the pirates do if we don't have anything they want?"

The cat leaps from his chair. We all watch as he prowls up the aisle between the seats, then leaps to Elodie's lap. He rubs his smushed face against hers. Elodie grips him tightly.

I sniff. "I doubt we'll find out."

Arun gives me a piercing look. "You think they'll let us go?"

"No, but I think they grabbed us because they *know* we have something they want. I just don't know what that is. You?" I point at Arun. "Elodie? Me? Not likely. The ship? Probably not. And they already have Leo." I lift a hand as they start babbling, cutting off their questions. "We need to find out who they are. Helva, can you get anything from their ship?"

"Nothing so far. Like I said, it's a second-hand military vessel. Not particularly well armed, but since we have *zero* weapons, that's good enough. They haven't attempted to communicate with us or anyone else. They appeared to be waiting out here, but that ship could have easily left the station when we did, then circled around. Their top speed is at least twice mine."

"Okay. They are either going to board us or tow us somewhere. I'd guess towing. Boarding a ship in space is a dangerous and messy prospect. Much easier to take us somewhere and wait us out. Or put us in an airdock and force our hatch. The fact that they haven't simply blasted us out of the sky or cracked us open makes me think they want one of us. Alive. That's good. As long as we're of value, we have a chance to escape."

I lock eyes with Arun, then with Elodie. "Do not mention Helva. An AI-helmed ship could be more valuable to them than any of us. In which case, we're all dead."

Arun pokes an icon in one of the holo screens. "You need to go silent, Helva."

"Aye, aye, Arun. I'm sending a code word to your holo-ring. You'll need it to reactivate me." The ship is all business now.

"Send it to Vanti too." Arun raises a brow at Elodie. "Do you want it?"

She flings up both hands. "Zark, no. I'd spill it faster than tea at a gossip party." The cat snakes out a paw and slaps her arm, so she resumes petting. "But I can fly us out if necessary."

Arun nods and points at me. "If you escape alone, Helva can fly you out."

Helva sighs loudly. "I can pretend to be a standard ship's system, but that will be *so* boring." So much for Helva's "all business" attitude.

"Boring but necessary." I pat the arm of my chair. I don't know if she can sense that, and I hope she doesn't think I'm condescending.

I close my eyes in self-disgust. Look at me, anthropomorphizing the shuttle software. Again. "I don't intend to escape alone. Unless I think I can come back and rescue you." With my data transmission complete, I don't have a competing mission from the CCIA.

The shuttle shudders.

"What was that?" Arun swings around to check the ship's systems.

"They locked on a tractor beam." Helva's dash lights flash. "They'd better not scratch my paint."

A laugh sputters out of Arun, but he chokes it back.

I cough. "Shouldn't the artificial gravity compensate for things like tractor beam grappling?"

"Of course. I did the shudder thing so you'd notice what's happening." A tiny spluttering hiss follows her words. Is Helva snickering?

"Next time, just tell us, okay?" Arun taps the dash. "Or ping me with an alert if you're running silent."

"I don't have to be completely silent, do I?" Her whiny tone switches to a robotic one. "I can pretend to be a computer."

"A computer wouldn't say it's pretending." I get up and head for the back of the ship. "What kind of survival gear do we have? EVA suits? Tondras? Anything?"

As Arun follows me to the back, Helva's voice moves to the rear speakers. She's still using the mechanical-sounding voice. "Tractor beam locked on. Forward momentum arrested. What are your instructions, captain?"

Arun closes his eyes for a second, then lets out a breath. "Please use your regular voice, Helva. I haven't heard a computer sound like that outside of an *Ancient TēVē* episode. And my instructions—" He breaks off and gives me a questioning look. "Do we try to break free? Or save the paint and shut down the engines?"

"Don't encourage her." I glance around the cargo hold. "Helva, can we break free?"

"Negative. Engine output is insufficient—"

"Then shut down and let's see what they do." I wait to see if Helva gives us a dramatic quake, but the ship doesn't even quiver. "Show me your gear."

Arun laughs as he uses a cutter to remove a metal band holding a cupboard closed. The Gagarian emblem embossed in the metal indicates its purpose—the weapons were locked away while we were on the planet. He presses his thumb against the reader and opens the door, revealing a case of stunners and blasters. "You show me yours, and I'll show you mine."

I ignore the little spurt of attraction that runs through me and pretend to take the comment at face value. "I'm armed, of course." I lean down and pull my mini-blaster from its ankle holster, then return it.

"How did you get that through Gagarian security?" Arun hands me the stunner I point at.

"That's my little secret."

"She left it here," Helva says in her normal voice. "I watched it for her."

Elodie appears in the space between the lavatory and the galley, still holding the cat. "I didn't see you hide it. Or retrieve it."

I fling up a hand. "Don't you share my secrets, Helva!"

Arun holds a stunner out to Elodie, but she doesn't take it. "No, thanks. I don't do weapons. That's why I have Vanti."

"Make sure you bring as many drones as you can hide on your person." I slip the stunner into the hidden pocket on my left side seam. My seemingly form-fitting clothing is constructed with some serious compression fabric and a little space between that and the exterior level. This allows me to hide a number of small items invisibly. It's the latest in Commonwealth tech. And although it makes me physically larger than I really am, I still look sleek. More importantly, it's super comfortable, so I love it.

Elodie puts Apawllo down and opens her large, pink suitcase, still strapped to the floor. I peer over her shoulder as she pulls hair ornaments and jewelry from it and puts them on.

"What's that one?" I point at an ornate clip with a gold lily.

"That has a drone and an on-board cam. So I can get two views of the same event. But it doesn't go with this outfit." She gestures to her pink coat and leggings.

"Mine, either." I look down at my black pants and jacket, suddenly regretting the fashion choice I was so happy with a moment before. Then I point at her. "Actually, that's perfect. Maybe not that one—I'd hate for you to lose it. But gimme something that would look out of place with this." I gesture to my clothing.

Elodie gives me a once over, then picks out a sparkly pin with a butterfly hovering over a daisy. The glittering, rainbow wings flutter, and its neon green eyes glow.

"No." I put my hands behind my back. "Not *that* out of place. Why do you have that? It's hideous."

She sighs as she pins the butterfly to her jacket. "It looks fabulous with this outfit. I would have worn it today, but I wasn't trying to be stealthy." With her rainbow-streaked hair and bright pink coat, the pin looks like it was made for this ensemble.

"Hey, when did you dye your hair?" Helva demands.

Elodie grins and flicks her holo-ring. "It's programmable." The rainbow changes back to blonde, then to brown, black, blue, through a whole array of individual colors and patterns. "Same tech as the clothing."

"Now you're making me wish I had hair," Helva grumps.

"Ladies, could we please focus?" Arun crosses the cargo hold, with matte gray fabric draped over his arm and a helmet dangling from his hand. "We've got one EVA suit. It's intended for repair work. Probably not going to do us any good in this situation."

I take the helmet and look inside, then hand it back to him. "See if you can hide it somewhere."

"Hide it?" He gestures to the interior of the cargo hold. The deck, bulkhead, and overhead are a clean, matte white material, flat and smooth. The cabinets on side bulkheads protrude from the walls and were obviously built specifically for their contents—EVA suit near the back hatch, tools, including the small selection of hand weapons, and open shelving for cargo. "Do you think this is a smugglers' ship with hidden compartments?"

I point at my ankle, where my mini-blaster resides. "I found a place to stash that."

The back of the EVA suit's storage pops open, revealing a dark space about waist high. "You mean like this hidden smuggler compartment?" Helva asks.

I shake my head sadly at Arun as I flash my holo-ring's light into the dark. "What else are you hiding?" The back wall curves, following the line of the shuttle's exterior. I grab the helmet and push it into the little cave. "Perfect. Put the suit away—they'll wonder why that compartment is empty. Gimme the weapons." Without looking, I reach over my shoulder.

Arun hands the suit and helmet to Elodie and starts pulling weapons from their nests. "Leave two—they'll wonder why we have none, but we can pretend we didn't expect to need more than two. Grab some food. And lock up the tools. Hopefully, they won't steal everything before we can escape."

"They'd better not try," Helva growls, and sparks fly from the tool compartment's handle.

Arun's eyes widen and he grimaces at me. "Let's keep the injuries to a minimum, Helva."

A heavy sigh blows from the speaker. "You're no fun."

We stash the remaining weapons and as much food as we can. While Arun closes the hidden compartment, I run the form-fitted tray that held those stunners and blasters through the recycler. The mostly empty shelf might look suspicious, but not as bad as eight empty, weapon-shaped slots.

"I think we're approaching our destination." Helva flashes an image into the center of the cargo hold. The cam zooms in on a small moon, curves dramatically around to the back side, then zooms even closer into a deep crater. An opening appears in the wall of the crater, large enough for several shuttles side-by-side. We approach and fly through an invisible barrier that glitters as we pierce it. The vid goes blank.

"Helva." Arun doesn't hide his exasperation well. "How much of that vid was real?"

"Oh, the moon is definitely real. We're on the dark side now. And we're approaching a crater. The rest was extrapolation."

"Put the live vid onscreen, please." Shaking his head, Arun walks toward the pilot's seat.

I follow, peering over his shoulder at the new vid. This one is grainier and not in color. The pirate ship isn't in evidence—it must be pushing us ahead of it. The crater grows larger as we approach.

"It's dark back here, of course." Helva illuminates a system map, showing our current location in relation to the sun. "I'm using non-visible wavelengths to create these images."

As we drop below the lip of the crater, its size becomes overwhelming. The ship's trajectory changes, and we begin descending vertically, as if loaded onto a giant elevator. The view rotates around the front of the ship until it's facing down.

"Ah. Not a cave, but a hidden moon base in the bottom of a crater!" Helva laughs. "This is so cool."

"This is not at all cool." I point at the holo. The rocks beneath the ship shimmer in the gray light, then drop. A seam appears across the center of the depressed area, then widens as doors slide sideways under the moon's surface. "Only the government could have built something this big. These aren't pirates."

ELEVEN

WE GAPE at the holo as our ship descends through the opening in the moon's floor. Arun grabs the back of the pilot's seat for balance.

"Close your eyes." Elodie demonstrates. "You can't feel a thing if you aren't watching."

"You didn't seem to like my simulated tractor beam grab, so I'm letting the artificial gravity compensate." Helva sounds aggrieved.

"It's fine." Arun releases the back of the chair. "Zark! We should have sent another message when they grabbed us."

I raise a brow at him. "You think we didn't?"

He looks at Elodie, then back at me. "We did? But you didn't shoot it out the window."

I smirk. "After the connection was calibrated, I didn't need to." My grin fades. "But it doesn't really matter. We're on our own here."

"What do you mean?" Elodie picks up Apawllo.

"The… people I sent that message to aren't going to swoop in and save us. My *company* expects me to take care of myself. And they aren't going to reveal the existence of that comm node. So unless we can get word back to the Commonwealth by another means, no one is riding to the rescue."

Elodie squeezes the cat so hard he struggles to escape. She immediately loosens her grip and leans down to whisper, "Sorry, fuzzy-wumpkins." When she looks up, tears shine in her eyes. "What are we going to do?"

Arun shoots a glare at me. "It's not that bad. Not to brag, but I know people. And I've done a lot for Gagarin's fledgling commercial enterprise. When we don't return to the *Ostelah*, Raynaud will file a report. My contacts on the planet will make sure it gets to the right people."

"Your contacts? Like Dima Sadiki?" I flick my holo-ring and toss a file to the front window. "I did a little research—"

"We're here!" Helva sings in a creepy voice. The ship judders, as if we've been dropped from a meter above the ground. "Sorry about that." She doesn't sound sorry. "Looks kind of creepy out there."

The blast panels over the forward windows slide aside and the holos dissolve so we can see out. Bright lights shine on us, making the rest of the space shadowy.

"Do you have a night vision setting?" I ask.

The background brightens, but it's still dark. "There's some kind of visual effect blocking me. They could have a whole army hidden in there."

"Helva, time for you to go silent. Open an external comm channel." Arun drops to his seat.

"No response to our comms, sir." The voice is Helva's but she's removed all emotion, making the tone flat and dead.

"Are we still in vacuum?" I ask.

"Negative. We passed through an atmospheric veil at the entrance to the base. The air outside the ship is thin but breathable."

"You have speakers on the outside, Helva?" I jut a thumb at the external bulkhead.

"Affirmative. External speakers on. Your mic is muted, captain."

Arun glances at a display that has popped up near his left leg. He pokes an icon and speaks in an official-sounding voice. "This is Captain Arun Kinduja of the trader *Ostelah Veesta*. I demand to know why you have taken my shuttle."

Ambient noises erupt from the speaker, then a deep voice replies. "You'll see soon enough, Ser Kinduja. Come on out, and we'll talk."

I shake my head.

"Negative. We will not exit the ship until you tell us who you are and your intentions." Arun makes a face at me as he says this. I give him a thumbs up.

The deep voice laughs. "You are in no position to negotiate. Come out."

Arun fingers his blaster, then flicks the mute button. "They didn't say anything about weapons. What's our best play?"

I clip the sleek silver hairpin Elodie gave me into my red hair, making sure the cam is on and recording. "I say we exit, carrying but not aiming our weapons. They will almost certainly relieve us of those, which is why we have others hidden." I point to my ankle, then back at the cargo hold. "Same reason we have obvious cams." I tap the clip.

"So they think they've disarmed us?" Arun pats his pockets. "I should grab another one."

I shake my head. "They'll find anything you have hidden on you. If they're any good, they'll find ninety-nine percent of *my* weapons." I shrug.

"But you don't need a weapon to be deadly." Elodie grins in a way that looks slightly unhinged. "That's what Triana told me."

I nod in acknowledgement of her statement. "True, but I'll never turn down a good blaster. We go out and surrender our weapons because we have no way to escape right now, and I don't want anyone getting hurt in a fight. We'll find out who they are and what they want, and hopefully a way to exit the situation before they send us to the gulag." I turn and head for the rear door. "It would probably be best if the cat stays aboard."

Elodie looks down at Apawllo. "What do you think?"

The cat tilts his head for a moment, then leaps to the dash of the ship. He stretches out in the corner formed by the top of the console and the front window, almost disappearing into the shadow.

"Perfect. Apawllo, guard the ship. Arun, Elodie, stay behind me.

Weapons out, aimed at the deck." I move to the rear of the ship and press the button to open the inner airlock. Nothing happens.

Arun pushes past me. "Sorry. I guess you aren't authorized for that." He waves his holo-ring at the panel, then presses the button. The inner hatch slides open, allowing us access to the small airlock. "Fix that, Helva."

"Fix what? Please rephrase that request, captain, to be more specific." Under Helva's dead tone, I detect a faint thread of humor. If she talks to the pirates, she is going to blow her cover.

Arun slaps the airlock's bulkhead. "Give Vanti access to all systems."

"Aye, sir. Vanti is now authorized to access all systems." The hatch behind us clangs shut, and air hisses. Then the ramp slowly rotates down, creaking ominously. Helva must be having a good time—it was silent when she opened it on Gagarin. As the panel begins hinging away from us, a dozen weapons make a metallic chi-ching sound.

Modern blasters don't chamber a round the way ancient projectile firearms did. But because the sound is embedded in the galactic conscience—thanks to centuries of entertainment vids—current weapons come equipped with a sound chip. When the gun is aimed, it plays a recording of that instantly recognizable sound, hoping to trigger panic in your target, encouraging them to lay down their own hardware.

It's pretty effective. Elodie squeaks. From the corner of my eye, I catch movement. Arun's hands fly out to the sides, as open as he can get them.

My stomach drops, and I go cold, but I squash the instinctive fear and activate a call to the others. "Arun. We aren't surrendering. Weapon out and aimed at the deck."

Arun's head turns toward me, then he tightens his grip and points the blaster a few meters ahead of his feet.

As the ramp opens, stuttering and clanging, our adversaries come into view. Ten people in full armor stand around the back of the ship, blasters pointed directly at us. Remembering our meeting with Aretha, I look for signs these might be projections, but find none. The ramp bangs on the plascrete, a puff of dust wafting up in its wake. The soldiers move forward a couple of paces and pause again.

"Welcome to Titov. Please surrender your weapons." It's the same voice as greeted us earlier, but this time it comes from behind the row of soldiers.

"Who are you?" I call, still holding my blaster across my hips. "Why did you take our ship?"

"Please, Agent Fioravanti, all will be answered. Surrender your weapons. I guarantee your safety."

"Oh, you do? And who guarantees your integrity?" I sweep my gaze across the open space, watching the soldiers. Through the implant, I warn the others. "Two approaching—four and eight o'clock. They'll come in from behind to get our guns."

Despite my warning, Elodie squeaks again when the two men appear on either side of the ramp. The one on the right pokes his gun toward us, reinforcing the demand we disarm. Keeping my gaze on the row of soldiers in front of us, I stoop and place my mini-blaster on the ramp. Arun does the same.

"And the others, Agent Fioravanti. Empty your secret pockets."

"I'm getting there." I pull the stunner on my ankle from its holster with two fingers and set it beside the blaster. The man on the right jerks his weapon at me again. I glare over my shoulder at him. "What? Use your words."

His low growl makes me want to smirk, but I maintain my poker face.

The same voice speaks again. "The garrote, Agent. And tranq ring."

"Ugh." I pull those items from my pockets as well as the switch blade and tiny case of poison darts. Then I stand. "Happy?"

"Hair stiletto?"

How does this guy know so much? Most of these concealed weapons are standard CCIA issue, but I don't know anyone else who hides a stiletto in their hair. Where are they getting their inside information?

I pull the blade from its hiding place, and a few locks come loose. I fight the urge to smooth them back as I set the sleek knife beside the other things. "I want these back when we leave. And you'd better not smudge the sheath."

The rank of soldiers parts, and a short figure steps between the middle two. "Welcome to Titov." The owner of the deep voice is broad and muscular, but his head tops out at mid-bicep on the nearest soldier. He wears light armor over his chest, a long-sleeved black shirt, and matching pants with multiple zippered pockets.

"You said that already." Arun takes a slow step forward, and when the armed men lower their weapons, he moves to the base of the ramp.

I hurry to catch up. "Stay behind me," I hiss through our audio connection.

His head shakes in a tiny negative.

The deep-voiced man holds both arms out wide, as if welcoming us to his domain. "I am Grigori Kalinovska Jones."

Arun crosses his arms. "So, Greg, care to tell us what this is all about?"

The short man laughs. "My, we are a feisty group. I was warned."

I move closer. "Warned? By who?"

"Whom."

"Really? You're correcting my Standard?" I mimic Arun's stance. Standing shoulder to shoulder at the base of the cargo ramp, we probably look like an advertisement for an action vid.

"Sorry. I used to teach *drugoyazyk*." My system translates this as "outside language" which is what the Gagarians call Standard. "Let's move somewhere more comfortable." As he says this, he turns and disappears into the darkness. Two of the soldiers fall in behind him. The rest wait.

I glance at Arun and raise a brow. He shrugs in return.

Elodie pushes between us. "I'm getting cold. I hope you have heat in this dump."

"You know I love some good snark but try not to piss off the guys holding the guns," I whisper through the audio.

"They haven't killed us yet, so they want something." Elodie takes a few steps after Grigori, then stops and speaks aloud. "Don't the lights work?"

A door opens. Light spills in, illuminating stacks of crates against the walls, tool chests, and a tarp draped over something bulky. Gregori pauses in the doorway and turns, peering between his two guards. "I also taught drama." His laugh follows him out the door.

Great, a dramatic pirate.

TWELVE

We follow Grigori down a dingy corridor. The light gray walls are scuffed near the bottom. Dented and broken conduits hang from the ceiling, and the dark floor bears numerous gashes and scrapes. The rubberized flooring muffles our footsteps. Cold, stale air gives me goosebumps. We pass through a heavy hatch, then turn a corner. It clangs shut behind us, the sound echoing through the long corridor.

At the end of that section, we walk through another hatch. Here the wall on our left is bumpy—as if the builders sprayed a sealant over natural stone. A door opens on the right, and a wave of warmth rolls over us as Grigori and his two goons move inside.

I pause at the doorway, assessing the room. It looks like a standard conference room, with a large plastek table surrounded by a dozen wheeled office chairs. The blank walls are a pale yellow and the overhead is in good repair. Carpet covers the floor. It looks newer than the rest of the base, as if the pirates have renovated this room. A familiar, dark-bearded man sits near the front of the room.

"Leo!" Elodie cries, rushing forward. The guards move aside. "Are you okay?"

Leo rises from his chair and envelops Elodie in a hug. "I'm fine."

"We were worried sick!"

"I'm fine!"

Elodie pulls back and slaps him softly on the arm. "You're fine? That's all you have to say?" She spins and advances toward Grigori. "Why did you kidnap him?"

The guards lift their weapons, using the barrels to block her.

Grigori puts out a hand and pushes the nearest man's weapon aside. "I didn't kidnap him. I rescued him." He raises his hands, cutting off our exclamations. "Please. Have a seat. Diya, get us some tea."

One of the soldiers near the door exits, grumbling under his breath. The rest have disappeared down the long hallway, leaving us with four guards—three men and a woman. The door swishes closed.

Grigori gestures at the table. "Sit down and let's talk."

Leo and Grigori sit on one side of the table. One of the soldiers stands behind his boss, while the other two move to the wall across the table from him. Their weapons are holstered, but their hands hover nearby. I note their alert stance—these three have some real training. The female soldier stands near the door, in front of the access panel.

Arun and Elodie take seats across from Leo, but I loiter near the door. I think I could take the woman guarding the exit, but the other three would draw on my friends before I could do anything. I could probably get her blaster and threaten her, but if these guys are as well trained as they seem, that won't deter them from shooting my friends.

As if she can hear my thoughts, the woman turns to look at me. Bright green hair sticks up from her head in a flattop cut so perfect it looks like a sports field. The severe style makes her angular features look like a skull. Her gaze flicks over my body, then locks on my eyes. She raises both green eyebrows as if in challenge, her lips curving in a tiny smirk. I turn away, giving her the side eye, then I focus on the group at the table.

Mostly. I'm not letting Green-hair out of my sight.

Leo folds his big, bony hands on the table. He's always been thin, but without his customary turban and robe, he looks gaunt. The black shirt hangs from his shoulders. But the smile is all Leo. His white teeth glint in his dark beard. "I'm so glad to see you guys!"

Elodie starts to say something, but Arun puts a hand on her arm. He gives Grigori a quick look, then gazes at Leo. "What's your status here?"

I mentally applaud Arun's question.

Leo glances at Grigori. "I'm a guest."

"A guest as in, 'hey, Leo, come hang with me'? Or a 'guest' who isn't allowed to leave?" Arun does air quotes around the second "guest."

"Leo can depart at any time." Grigori claps a hand on Leo's shoulder. "We are old friends, and he is always welcome to come hang with me, as you say."

I initiate a call to Leo's audio implant. My system replies with a "not available" indicator. I try Arun, and it goes through immediately. "I can't connect to Leo's comms."

Arun gives a tiny nod but doesn't reply. He pushes back his chair and says to Leo, "Great. Why don't we head home, then?"

The man behind Grigori takes a half step forward, his hand dropping to his holstered weapon. Arun freezes.

Grigori lifts a hand. "That is not necessary."

The soldier behind him casts an unreadable look at the back of Grigori's head—probably querying via their own comm system—then steps back against the wall.

Arun scoots his chair in again and rests his forearms on the table, staring hard at Leo. "You're allowed to leave, but we aren't?"

A broad smile spreads across Grigori's face. "Now you get it!"

An icy wave chills me, despite the warmth of the room. Did Leo sell us out?

"I don't." Elodie points at Grigori. "Are you trying to tell us Leo came with you willingly? That he helped you lure us out here to rescue him, so you could kidnap us?"

Grigori tips a hand on edge. "Lure, kidnap—these are such ugly words."

"I'm not sure 'willingly' is entirely accurate, either." Leo grimaces at Grigori, then he turns back to Arun and Elodie. "Grigori's friends—" He frowns as he says the word, his gaze flicking to the green-haired woman then back. "He sent someone to bring me here. It wasn't what I'd call an 'invitation.' Kidnapping is ugly but probably accurate."

"To*may*to, to*mah*to." Grigori rocks his hand again. "Yleni made sure you arrived in an expedient and trouble-free matter." He beams at the woman by the door.

She nods like the Ice Dame at a public appearance—regal, cold, intimidating.

I pledge to myself: before this is over, Yleni's smug attitude is going down.

"But if you're free to leave, why didn't you? You could have come back—if you'd asked, we would have flown out here. You should have at least let us know you weren't injured or dead." Tears glitter in Elodie's eyes, but she doesn't shed them.

Arun leans back, crossing his arms. "If I had to guess, I'd say Leo and Greg go way back, but they aren't necessarily 'friends.' Greg didn't know if Leo would help him willingly, so he sent Yleni to make sure he came. Once he got here, Leo agreed to help."

"Bravo!" Grigori jumps to his feet, applauding.

I watch Leo's face. He's not smiling, and his spine is stiff. I activate my audio link to Arun. "Saying Leo was compelled to help might be more accurate."

Arun grunts, then replies via the same channel. "Agreed. He's being coerced. We need to figure out how."

"Find out what they want, first."

Arun turns his chair to face the short man who now stands at the end of the table, between me and my friends. "What do you want?"

Grigori throws his arms wide. "I want freedom for the people of Gagarin!"

"Sorry, Greg, that might be a bit beyond my capabilities."

"It's not really your help we're requesting." Grigori swings around and points a finger at me. "It's hers."

THIRTEEN

TIME TO THINK FAST. Grigori thinks I can help him, and he knows I'm an agent. Does he know who I really work for? Leo doesn't. He might suspect, but I have never confirmed my CCIA status. I lift both hands, palms up. "My reach is significantly smaller than Ser Kinduja's. I'm a freelance bodyguard for a net star. I don't even have access to the SK2 leadership anymore."

Grigori snaps his fingers. Yleni, still across the entrance from me, swings to face me head on. The two men behind Elodie and Arun take a step closer to my friends.

Leo grimaces and shakes his head. "Trust me, if you want Vanti to help, threatening her friends is not the way to do it."

"There are no threats!" Grigori mirrors my stance, with his hands out, his feet planted. "My friends, you are in no danger from me. I humbly request your assistance."

I assess my options. I could grab Grigori and use him as a human shield before Yleni could pull her blaster, but that leaves Elodie, Arun, and Leo unprotected. I could grab Yleni's weapon first, then use it to hold Grigori hostage. That might allow us to exit the room, and possibly get us to the ship, but there's no way to ensure we could escape their tractor beam.

At this point, my best action is to gather more intel. "What exactly do you want me to do?"

Grigori rubs his hands together and jerks his head at the table. "Come. Sit. We'll have tea. Where's Diya?" He claps once, then pulls out a chair. "Please. Sit."

With a quick glance at Yleni, I cross the room and sit on the lightly cushioned seat. I rotate my hips a little to test how easily it swivels—I want to make sure I can get out fast, even with the arm rests. Easing the chair a few centimeters farther from the table, I lean forward to make the distance less obvious. "What do you want?"

Grigori waves my question aside and speaks into his wrist device, demanding Diya return with the tea. I cast a quick look at the goons behind Grigori. I thought they were communicating via audio implants, but perhaps they don't have that tech? Or is Grigori using his wrist device to make me think they don't have the tech?

Sometimes analyzing all of the possibilities dumps me into a swirling vortex of maybe. Time to ignore that and learn as much as possible.

Diya returns, pushing a metal cart. An old-fashioned tea service, complete with porcelain cups and tiny silver spoons sits on top. A lower shelf holds two trays of pastries. Diya—a huge, brawny man with wild, graying hair and a coarse, shaggy beard that reaches the middle of his chest—serves the tea. His pinky finger extends as he pours, then he uses the silver tongs to drop cubes of sugar into each cup without asking what we want. Arun gets milk and one cube—I get black tea with four sugars.

"Do you have any water?" I nudge the saucer with a finger. "I'm not much of a hot-beverages gal."

"Diya, water." Grigori snaps his fingers.

Diya drops the tray of pastries on the table with a thud and lumbers away, muttering under his breath. My translator says something about "philistines."

"Please, enjoy." Our host takes a flaky, sticky-looking wedge covered in chopped nuts.

I fold my arms, declining the sweets. "I don't have time for tea, Greg. I want to know what you want."

Grigori chuckles. "You have time for whatever I want you to have time for. And I want tea." While he eats his pastry, he makes comments about the weather.

We're on a moon. What weather is he even talking about?

Diya returns with a dirty glass full of cloudy liquid. I accept the glass with a gracious smile and thanks. No point in upsetting the giant now that I know he's prickly. He smiles, his snaggle teeth showing amid his scraggly beard. The five teardrops tattooed under his eye crinkle with his smile lines, and he whispers, "You're welcome."

Finally, Grigori wipes his fingers on a napkin and pushes his plate away. "And now, business." He taps his wrist device, and a projector embedded in the table lights. "At one time, I was a respected member of Gagarin society. Before the current regime took control, I had many factories that created goods for the people." Three dimensional images pop up, each object rotating like an item on display for sale, then replaced by the next one. A series of furniture, vehicles, farm equipment, and some mechanical things I don't recognize appear and disappear. "Kalinovska Jones was one of the largest manufacturers in the system. When Fyodo Salahnovich came to power, I lost everything. Seized by the state."

The holo changes to a view of the planet, rotating slowly. Various spots light briefly, then fade out. "My companies were consolidated with others, my employees' wages were cut, my suppliers were decimated, everything in ruins. I left with some of my most trusted associates." He gestures to the armed men and Yleni. "My company was not the first, of course. We saw what happened to others, so we brought our families and as much wealth as we could consolidate and moved out here."

"You didn't build this base." I make it a statement, not a question.

"No. This was a government facility, mothballed many decades ago. By Kalinovska Jones, as it turns out." He smirks. "I've used my own fortune to keep it functional. Which has been quite expensive, since I also needed to keep it secret. But worthwhile when the time came."

"Exiled to an abandoned moon base. Got it. What do you think I can do for you? I'm not a revolutionary." I fold my arms, suppressing the urge to check my remaining hidden weapons.

You didn't think I gave up everything, did you?

He smiles as he shakes his head, as if he finds me amusing. I make a mental note to take him down a peg too. "I don't need a revolution. I need an assassin. The revolution will take care of itself. I want you to kill Fyodo Salahnovich."

A chill runs down my spine. Grigori's cheerful, friendly demeanor has disappeared. His tiny stature doesn't make his stone-faced statement any less threatening. This guy wants the Gagarian Secretary General assassinated, and he wants me to do it.

My gaze flicks to Elodie, Arun, and Leo. And unless I'm very much mistaken, he will hold my friends hostage to ensure I do his bidding.

Trying to buy some time to think, I sip from my glass and nearly spew the water across the table when I taste the vile stuff. I catch Diya smirking at me from his corner. I guess I didn't win him over after all. I swallow, trying not to gag, then pat my lips with a napkin. "Assassinating a sitting head of state is not something a foreigner can just walk in and do. I have no idea where he lives or what protection he has. Getting close enough to take him out would take years of planning and a support system to put intelligence operatives in place. There's no way a single agent can pull this off."

"I'm so disappointed to hear you say that, Agent Fioravanti." Grigori folds his hands on the table. "Because my analysts say it's the only way to take him out. That a larger enterprise would undoubtedly be compromised and therefore fail. A single agent means a single point of failure."

"Exactly." I stab a finger at him. "If I tried and failed—which I would undoubtedly do—then you have no back up plan."

He smiles gently, as if to a child. "Then we get another agent and try again."

The cold in my soul crystalizes to ice. "I'm not the first, am I? How many times have you already tried?"

He shrugs and frowns at the ceiling, as if the answer is written there. "Fifteen? Twenty, maybe? But none of them were the infamous Vanti."

FOURTEEN

I SLIDE down the door of the "room" Grigori has allotted to me. The now familiar rubbery coating covers the walls, but they are smooth, as if a giant knife sliced sections from the rock. The thick stone effectively cut off communication via our audio implants the moment they shoved me inside. Was that intentional or a lucky side effect?

The tiny compartment holds a narrow bed, a tiny sanitation cubicle, and an ancient computer system. Yleni said it contains data from the eighteen failed attempts on Fyodo Salahnovich's life—all of them undertaken in the last three years on an escalating schedule. I tried to convince Grigori launching another attack a mere two weeks after the previous one failed would be a recipe for disaster. But he isn't interested in waiting a few years for Salahnovich's security to get complacent.

Elodie, Leo, and Arun have been sequestered somewhere else—they could be right next door for all I know. I thud the back of my head gently against the door, trying to imagine a way out of this mess.

After a few fruitless minutes on the floor, I get up and look at the computer console. A large circular button sits flush with the front of the console, below a dark screen. I can't read the Gagarian beside it, and with my holo-ring disconnected from any net, a visual translator is not available. I try sounding out the words, but Gagarian uses different letters, and I'm only guessing at them. With a shrug, I press the button.

Something hums, the flat, green screen brightens, and a tiny line blinks in the top left corner.

"Computer, I need a summary of your current data, organized chronologically, oldest to newest."

The little line continues to blink.

I try rewording my request but get no response. I ask for a list of files. Nothing. That smug green line continues to blink. The thing isn't responding to any commands. It's old, so maybe it doesn't do voice.

I tap the screen. Nothing happens.

Crossing my arms, I take a step back to give the thing my best death glare. I know it won't help, but it might make me feel better. Then I notice an open slot beneath the desk. The base of the slot rolls forward in response to my touch, revealing an ancient keyboard in the flat drawer.

The keyboard is in Gagarian, of course.

I pound a fist against the door. "Hey. I need help with this computer!"

I listen but don't hear anyone moving. I pound again.

A key rattles in the archaic lock, and the knob turns. The door swings out, revealing Yleni's skull-like face, made even more unattractive by a sneer. "You need help?" The last word drips with disdain.

Oddly, her voice is unaccented, and she's speaking Standard. Did Yleni study in the Commonwealth? Maybe I can turn her.

"Yes. I don't know how to work this obsolete device." I gesture at the blinking green line.

She looks at the open keyboard drawer, then at me. "You type your query in and it responds."

I lift both hands. "I don't know your language."

With a sullen glare, she closes the door and locks us both into the room. "Don't try anything. I'd love a chance to put you down." She pats her weapon—a stunner not a blaster. She must have exchanged the deadly weapon for this one when Grigori put her on guard duty. They don't want her accidentally killing the operative—or the hostages, I hope.

Yleni juts her chin at the computer. "I'll tell you what to type. What do you want to know?"

I repeat my original request. She frowns for a second. "Right, try this." She follows that with a string of sounds. My translator converts them to Standard letters, but I have no idea which symbol on the keyboard corresponds to the names.

"Not helping." I raise both hands and step away from the machine, to the corner near the sanitation cubicle. "Can you just type it in?"

She glares at me, her eyes narrowing, then she points at the cubicle. "Get in."

I don't bother protesting—it's exactly what I'd do. I open the cubicle and step inside, my knees banging against the toilet. I turn as she shuts the door, and the interior lights come on, illuminating the dingy plastek sink and soap-scummed shower. Fortunately, the tiny room doesn't stink.

Yleni's voice cuts through the flimsy plastek door. "Come look."

I open the door, and the cubicle's lights flicker off. Data scrolls up the green screen, too fast to read. Yleni touches a key, and the flow stops. I peer at the glowing letters. "I still can't read it."

"Lazy *postoronniy*. You come to my planet without learning the language?"

"I have a very effective translator—but it requires net access." The visual translator requires access. I don't tell her the audio is self-contained. Maybe I'll overhear something useful if they think I can't understand them. I make a mental note to check with Arun and Elodie when I see them. We need to make sure our stories match.

"Back in the sani."

I refrain from rolling my eyes as I step back inside. "You don't have to lock me in here—there's nowhere for me to run."

"My orders are clear. You are to stay in this room."

I go in, leaning against the wall while she fiddles with the machine.

"You can come back out." She steps away from the screen and points. "I have activated the translator. Do you know the *drugoyazyk* keyboard? I can't change the markings on the keyboard, but if you know where the letters are, you can type in your own language, now."

"I can figure it out. Thanks." I glance at the screen, then turn back to her. "How did you learn such fluent *droo-goy-zik*?" I mis-pronounce the word on purpose.

She rolls her eyes. "I studied in the Commonwealth, of course. Gagarin has many operatives trained in your land. You let anyone go to school."

"And that's a bad thing?"

"It's a security risk. You must see that."

I shrug. "Sure, but most of the time, people who study in the Commonwealth decide to stay. Like Leo."

"Leweians are not as strong as Gagarians. They are tempted by your easy ways and loose morals." The words sound like a quote—and as if she doesn't quite believe them.

I shrug. "It's nicer there. Gagarin is cold, the gravity is heavier, and the government is—"

"Oppressive. But we will fix that. *You* will fix that." She stomps into the hallway and slams the door.

I shake my head and rub my eyes. Perfect. A true believer. I thought someone who had experienced the better lifestyle of the Commonwealth might be easy to turn to my side, but Yleni would take more patience than I have right now.

I spend the rest of the day paging through the data on the computer. As Grigori said, eighteen credible attempts have been made on Salahnovich's life. Seventeen by his people and another one by an unaffiliated Gagarian.

That last one was a Commonwealth sleeper operative activated after the most recent revolution. But I'm not telling Grigori that.

All of Grigori's attempts were carefully planned, multi-pronged campaigns involving between five and twenty people. Most of the participants were rounded up and executed. I make a note of Grigori's operatives who escaped the purges. Only their code names are listed in the system, but Grigori must know how to reach at least one of them.

Countless other attempts never came near completion. They're all carefully documented in this computer system. I have to give Grigori points for thorough research.

The key tumbling softly, carefully, in the lock snaps my attention from the screen. By the time the door opens, I'm flattened against the wall, ready to attack my assailant.

"Dinner." It's Diya. The rolling cart bangs against the door frame, then rolls into the room. The bearded man eyes me as I step away from the wall, then lifts the tray. "Where do you want this?"

I look around the room. The small table in front of the computer monitor is littered with scraps of paper and a tablet. The only other horizontal surface is the bed. I point at it. "There, I guess."

"Step away from the door." He waits until I retreat to the computer chair, then deposits the tray on the bed. He returns to the cart, his hand hovering over a thermal carafe. "You want tea?"

The glass of water on the cart looks identical to the one I had earlier. It might even be the same dirty glass. Luckily, the water in my sani cubicle is potable. "Sure, I'll try the tea. No sugar, please."

He pauses, then shrugs and pours some tea into a large mug. With another sideways look, he drops two cubes of sugar on a saucer and deposits it beside the tray. "You'll thank me later."

"Thank you now."

He gives me another unreadable look, then backs to the door, pulling the cart. "I like you. Too bad you'll be dead soon."

Everything about that statement is chilling. "You don't think I can pull this off?"

He nods at the computer. "They didn't, and they trained for months."

I press my lips together. Based on what I've read so far, that's true.

But none of them had my training. Even the Commonwealth spy had been woefully inexperienced. Plus, he'd gotten complacent over the years. His lack of physical fitness should have disqualified him from the mission, but maybe his handlers didn't know. "Any advice?"

"Don't do it." He backs out and closes the door. The lock tumbles, clicking loudly this time.

FIFTEEN

THE OVERHEAD LIGHTS GO OUT. My green computer screen provides a soft glow, but the sudden darkness snaps me out of my stupor. I've been sitting in front of this thing for hours. I shut off the screen and let my eyes adjust to the darkness. The walls glow a pale yellow—some kind of emergency lighting? Pushing back the chair, I rise to do some stretches.

Limbered up, I listen at the door for a few moments, then pick the lock.

You didn't think an old-style tumbler was going to keep me in, did you? And I told you I had a few tools still hidden.

I slide the lockpicks back into the sole of my shoe and ease the door open. The hallway is dark, with that faint glow from the walls. Only on the rough side—maybe an effect of the stone dampened by the coating? I touch the rubbery surface, then glide down the hall, activating my audio implant.

I pass a couple of doors before my system pings with Elodie's signal. I unlock the closest door and ease it open. A faint snuffling snore reaches my ears. "Elodie?"

She mumbles something, but I only get the end: "...feed the cat."

Zark! We left Apawllo on the shuttle.

I pull the door closed and continue. Three doors later, Arun's signal pings and connects immediately. "Vanti?"

"Roger. I'm opening your door." I pick the lock and ease the door open but don't enter. If this isn't Arun, I'd prefer to avoid a blow to the head.

Arun appears in the open doorway. "How'd you get out?"

I grin as I slide my tools into their hiding place. "I have my ways. Wanna go exploring with me?"

"Always." He pushes the door closed and follows me down the hall. "I don't suppose you have a spare set of lock picks?"

I frown at him, unseen in the dim light. "You know how to use them? Picking locks is not typically part of the top-lev educational curriculum."

He snorts, the sound soft and intimate in the dark. "I'm a Kinduja. We aren't typical top-levs."

"Good point. I can get you a set when we feed the cat."

I feel more than see his head snap toward me. "I forgot about him."

"Poor kitty."

"I'll bet the *poor kitty* has already ransacked the shuttle and figured out how to work the AutoKich'n."

Stifling a snort of amusement, I put out my arm, stopping him at the corner. The hallway ahead of us is dark, but a glow emanates from the branch to the right. I pull the drone from my hairpin and send it down the hall, setting the vid holo to the lowest possible brightness. The buzz seems loud, but these things have a volume similar to an insect. Of course, there aren't very many insects on a defunct moon base.

As if to prove me wrong, another faint buzz approaches from the darkness behind us. I glance away from my screen. "What is that?"

Elodie's call signal pings and connects. "It's me. How'd you get out?"

"Trade secret. How are you calling us with all this rock in the way?" I pat the wall beside me.

"Trade secret. Just kidding. I'm using the drone to relay the call. I see you!"

I squint into the darkness but can't find the drone. "Cool. We're checking out the base."

"And feeding the cat," Arun says.

"He's fine." Elodie chuckles. "I taught him to open the lock on the cat food container. Just in case. And his water dish is connected to the shuttle's life support system. Helva will take care of him."

I give her a thumbs up and return to my own drone controls. The device has moved into the lighted portion of the base, but there's no movement. "I wish we could get into their comms and see where everyone is."

"I can do that." Arun flicks his holo-ring, the glare temporarily blinding me. He dials it back. "Sorry."

The afterglow makes it hard to see my screen, but after a few blinks I adjust. "Any idea where Leo is? And whose side he's really on?"

"He's on our side." Elodie's voice is hard and flat, as if daring me to suggest otherwise. "Grigori threatened him."

"How do you know?" Arun asks. I mentally applaud the question. He and Leo don't have as much history, so maybe Elodie won't get offended by him asking.

"He told me. He visited me this evening, before lights out."

"He's free to wander the facility, but he didn't let you out." I guide my drone farther into the base. The hallways are lit, but not to full power. Doors are closed, and all is quiet. Do Space Pirates have a bedtime curfew?

"He couldn't. Grigori's people have our ship locked down. He said if we can disable the tractor beam, we can get away, but he's being watched. Plus, he doesn't know how to do it."

Arun grunts. "It probably isn't as easy as the adventure vids make it look. But I can take a crack at it."

"Bogie, on screen. Coming this way." I stab a finger at my holo-screen, which seems criminally bright in the dark hallway. We retreat a few meters from the intersection. I unzip my jacket and use it to shield the light. The guy—Olav, I think—glances down our corridor, then turns and heads up one of the lighted ones. A door opens, and he steps inside.

I send the drone down the hall at top speed, rotating it to peek inside the room. Just before the door shuts, I catch sight of what looks like a lounge.

"See if you can go under the door." Arun's voice comes through the audio implant, but his breathing is loud in my ears. His body gives off enough heat to make me aware of the chill of the corridor—the temperature seems to have dropped. They probably turn down the heat as well as the lights.

"This is a moon base. Won't the doors be airtight?" Elodie asks.

"No." I send the drone to the floor. "There are airtight bulkheads—those big double doors we went through on the way to the cells. They're all open now but will slam shut in the event of a decompression. The internal doors are standard, hollow-core plastek—like you'd have in your house on Kaku. Except probably cheaper, because this is a Gagarian government base."

Arun chuckles softly. "If it were a Commonwealth base, they'd be cheaper but more expensive to produce."

I roll my eyes, even though he can't see it. And even though he's right.

The drone slides through the gap under the door, then rises slowly. The audio picks up some chatter, so I swivel the view. This must be the goons' lounge. Olav sits at a table with three other almost indistinguishable men. They hold cards, and stacks of small, smooth rocks sit beside each player's elbow. The guy on the right tosses a handful of the stones to the center of the table and says something in Gagarian, too low to pick up. The next guy grunts and tosses a few rocks to the middle.

I turn the drone to check the rest of the room. Yleni and Diya are not here, but the rest of the soldiers we saw at the landing pad must be. "Any idea how many guys Grigori has?"

"Leo said there's ten," Elodie says.

"Good work. Ten including Grigori and Yleni? Or—"

"Ten people here, total. Families are offsite, so only the fighters remain. And there's a larger network on the planet. Leo said the repeated attempts on the secretary general have whittled down their numbers."

"You're telling me." I maneuver the drone out of the room. "Four guys playing poker, plus the guy on the couch watching the vid. That means there are five others unaccounted for. Plus Leo."

"He's on our side."

"If you say so." I give Arun a look he probably can't see, and he doesn't respond. "There must be a control room somewhere. Someplace to monitor the base as well as communications with the planet."

"You think they have someone there twenty-four seven?" Arun whispers.

"That term doesn't really apply on a moon base. But no. With only ten people, I'd set up automated alerts and have someone on call. Probably one of those guys in the lounge. Everyone else is likely asleep since they seem to have designated this 'night.'"

I sit against the wall and stretch out my legs. "What do you see, Elodie?"

"Just you. If I send the drone farther, I'll lose contact with you guys. I tried earlier, and my signal cuts off right beyond where you are."

"Nice work." I should have thought to send out my drone.

Arun touches my shoulder. "I can let her out."

I shake my head violently. We don't need Elodie the wild card running loose.

"Nah, I'll stay here." She yawns.

"Can you do an auto recon run with that thing?" I send my drone into the next room, but it's dark. There are too many closed doors along this corridor. This base must have housed thousands in its prime.

"Sure. It'll take a couple of hours. If you mark your cell on the map,

I'll have it swing by and deliver the files to you before returning to me."

A file appears in my inbox. I open it to find a map of this corridor. I count back and mark my door—it's at the far edge of the charted area. "Thanks, Elodie. See you tomorrow." I send the drone on its way.

The drone will navigate the complex, using infrared, photo, and echo sensors to map the entire facility. If Elodie used the most intrusive settings, it will fly under doors to map any rooms along the way. The drone works independently, returning to its origin when it has covered the entire place. There are systems that can be set to keep a drone from entering, but Grigori doesn't seem to have expected this kind of intrusion.

"She probably won't find the control room." I lean against the wall as my own drone continues on its path. "That will likely have a sealed door. So, unless someone happens to wander in or out at the right time…"

Arun slides down the wall to sit beside me, his arm touching mine. "Should we do some more checking on our own?" He yawns.

I bump my shoulder against his arm. "Stop that. My drone is just about at the end of its reach. Maybe we should go back to our rooms and let them do their thing. I can stretch out the planning of this mission a few days, I think." I fight back a yawn. "And Apawllo won't starve, so I think we can—" Another yawn cuts me off.

Arun rises and reaches down to me. In the glow of my holo-ring, only his well-manicured fingers are visible. I grip his hand and let him pull me to my feet, stumbling a bit when I hit vertical. He catches my shoulder with his left hand, our clasped right hands trapped between us, the glow of my holo-ring muffled against his chest. His free hand slides off my shoulder and down my back, warm through my jacket and shirt. His breath tickles my temple, and his breathing sounds fast and shallow. His warm, slightly spicy scent wraps around me, both comforting and arousing.

"We should go back to our rooms," he whispers into my hair. "If they spot one of those drones, they'll come looking."

Way to kill the mood, Kinduja. I shift sideways, releasing his hand

and moving away from his arms. "Good thought. Let's go." I turn and hurry away.

"Vanti…"

Ignoring his laughing undertone, I unlock his door and swing it wide with a flourish. "Good night, Ser Kinduja." Then I stalk away.

SIXTEEN

THE NEXT MORNING, Yleni takes me back to the conference room for breakfast. She makes me walk in front of her but doesn't hold onto my arm like she did yesterday. I might be gaining her trust. And no, I won't feel at all bad about breaking it. It's what a good agent does.

Well, I might feel a twinge of remorse, but I've learned to suppress that.

Diya lays his omnipresent tea in the center of the large table, fussing over the placement of spoons and napkins. Another tray of pastries and a huge bowl of white stuff join the tea. "Yogurt." Diya shoves a smaller bowl and spoon at me, then leaves me alone in the room.

I scoop some of the yogurt into my bowl along with a handful of the berries hidden behind the stack of baklava and bear claws. Then I pour some tea into the mug Diya brought my room and add two cubes of sugar. Diya was right—the dark tea is bitter, even for me. Taking my meal, I retreat to the far end of the table where I can watch the door.

I've just started on my surprisingly tasty breakfast when the door opens again. Grigori enters, followed by Yleni and five of the interchangeable thugs. They all wear tight shirts over their big brawny muscles and carry an assortment of dangerous-looking weapons. Of the group, I've pegged Yleni as the most dangerous. The others have numbers on their side, but I could take them.

Except maybe Diya. He could poison my food, and I'd be dead. Or he could sit on me, and I'd be dead.

Fortunately, Grigori wants me alive.

While the thugs dish up their breakfasts, Grigori takes a cup of tea and settles in beside me. "How goes the research?" He looks tired, his eyes bloodshot and his skin pale. A faint bruise on his cheekbone near his eye adds to the unkempt appearance.

"You know this is impossible, right?" I yawn. Normally, I'd hide any hint of weakness from an adversary, but I want Grigori to underestimate me. I blink rapidly, then sip my tea.

"If I keep trying, I will eventually succeed."

"If this were a skill that could be learned, I might agree with you. But assassinating a political authority isn't a single skill. His security people are at least as good as I am, and they have the home team advantage." They aren't anywhere near as good as I am, but the lie trips easily off my tongue.

"I have complete faith in you, Vanti. I've heard such good things!"

I work very hard to stay incognito. "From who?"

"Whom."

I grit my teeth. "Whom'd you hear it from?"

He gives a sad head shake at my mangled contraction. "A number of reliable sources. Most recently, your friend Gary Banara."

My jaw spasms. Gary Banara was a classmate at the academy. But the last time I saw him, he had defected to the Leweian government. I thought he was in prison on Kaku.

Grigori stands, leaving his half-drunk tea on the table. "You have until Thursday. Yleni, please return our guest to her room."

"Thursday?!" I yank my arm away from Yleni's grip. "I can't plan an assassination in two days!"

Yleni pulls her stunner and points it at me. "Don't make me use this. I'd have to use Diya's food trolley to roll you back to your cell, and he doesn't like me transporting bodies on it."

I give her a dirty look, throw another one at Grigori, and stomp out of the room.

"Wrong way." Yleni grabs my arm again. "Your cell is that way." She glances away as she jerks her head toward my room.

I give her my most condescending glare. I could take her down, stash her in one of these empty rooms, and get to the control room before anyone knew she was missing. But then what? Without Arun, I don't think I can disable the tractor beam. I could wreck stuff, but any physical damage would probably activate safety protocols that would make escape harder, not easier. I could stash Yleni, run back and unlock Arun and Elodie, then go to the control room, but we might run into one of the thugs.

As if in response to my thoughts, the conference room door opens and two of the thugs saunter out. "You need some help, Yiny?" They both laugh.

Yleni gives me an icy stare, not looking at the thugs. "In your dreams, idiot." Her glare seems to demand feminine solidarity.

Since taking down all three of them at once would probably alert the others, I decide to cooperate. Besides, I do feel some solidarity—being the only woman in a male-dominated career field can be difficult. I can't let these morons think Yleni can't do her job. I let my shoulders droop as I slouch past the thugs, Yleni closing in behind me.

Of course, letting the thugs underestimate my skills will probably be useful later too.

When we get to my room, she opens the door and follows me inside. "Thanks for that."

I frown. "For what?"

"Those idiots think women can't do this."

"Women are just as good at kidnapping and intimidation as men!"

"I know, right?" She does a double take, as if she's reassessing my sincerity. Then she nods once. "You aren't so bad for a *postoronniy* wimp."

"Thanks. Right back at ya." I turn to the computer so she can't see my smirk. When the door snicks shut, I check over my shoulder to make sure she actually left. That woman moves like a ninja.

A knock at the door brings my head around. "Come in," I call in a sing-songy voice, as if they won't enter if I don't. In my opinion, half of surviving captivity is attitude—which is one hundred percent situational. In this location, with these captors, pretending I'm here by choice is my current strategy. Since Grigori has been playing that fiction since he grabbed Leo, I figure it's the best way to get the guards to relax their vigilance.

The door opens, and Elodie saunters in, followed by Diya with his cart. "I convinced Grigori he should let us eat together. I invited Arun, but Diya says he's otherwise occupied." She takes a seat on the bed as if it's a throne.

I guess Elodie is using my strategy, too. Or she's bought the fiction. With Elodie, it's hard to tell.

Diya places the cart in front of Elodie, where it blocks easy access to the door, then whisks the covers off a pair of plates. Steam wafts out, carrying scents of grilled meat, garlic, fresh bread, and lemon. "*Grick* chicken with *pheeta* cheese." He stacks the two dish covers and backs out of the room. "Enjoy."

"His Standard is remarkably good." Elodie picks up her fork and pokes at her lunch. "And these tomatoes look delicious. Do you think he grows them here?"

I snag a piece of warm flat bread and inhale. Yeasty, toasty, delicious. I don't normally eat bread, but even I can't resist this. "I don't care where he gets his tomatoes, as long as he serves them to us." I shovel a pile of the salad onto my plate, add a heap of the fragrant meat, and dump the garlicky white sauce on top. With the first bite, I moan with pleasure. "This is good."

Elodie gives me a puzzled look. "It is yummy."

I connect an audio call. "I'm sure they're listening. Don't talk about anything except the food."

"Won't that be suspicious?" She blinks innocently at me and speaks aloud. "Do you think we'll get to leave soon?"

Elodie is even easier to underestimate than I am. I should take notes. "They want me to do that *little job* for them. I'm sure they'll let you go as soon as I take care of it. Or get killed."

Alarm crosses Elodie's face. "Don't say that! You're—"

I cut her off before she reveals anything. Every time I think she's a gazillion times smarter than she pretends, she crushes that belief with a stupid error. "This mission is impossible. If I don't get killed, I'll certainly be sent to the gulag. Getting the job done might be possible. Getting out undetected is—let's call it unlikely."

Through the audio, I remind her. "I want them to think I'm less competent than they've been told. Help me out, will you?"

"Sure." She chews and swallows, then speaks again. "Maybe it will be like that time on Armstrong—when everything just accidentally worked out. Or the mission on Sally Ride when Ty saved your bacon. Or that trip to—" At my death glare, she stops with a twinkling grin. "You're really lucky."

"Thanks." If they're watching us as well as listening, we're screwed. But I haven't detected any cams. "Any idea what Arun is up to?"

She shakes her head. "Grigori didn't tell me. Just that's he's busy. Why? Do you think he abandoned us?"

My stomach drops in alarm. Could he have bribed Grigori to release him and left us behind? "He wouldn't!"

Elodie sizes me up. "We don't know him that well. Maybe he set us up in the first place."

Could she be right? We met only a few weeks ago. Most of what I know about him is from stories R'ger—his uncle—told us. And R'ger loves embroidering the truth, as he calls it. I thoroughly researched his background before we joined him, but maybe I didn't look as deep as I should have. Based on his top-lev status, I shouldn't have had to dig too far.

Right, Vanti, keep telling yourself that. If you didn't look too deep, it's because you like him, and you didn't want to find a reason to decline his invitation.

Did I compromise my mission due to my personal feelings? I pulled his file from the CCIA databases, of course. Typical junior-top-lev stuff. He "ran away" from the family and joined a shipping company on Sally Ride. After working his way to the top, he bought out the owner, using the credits he'd accumulated over the years.

The "top-levs starting from nothing" narrative has always grated on my nerves. Even my friend Triana didn't start from nothing. She had a great education that allowed her to earn scholarships after her first term at the Techno-Inst. And she started with enough funds to survive that first term. Plus, her mother secretly arranged a roommate for her. Arun landed on Sally Ride with a pilot's license and a nice little nest egg to start. Their "nothing" was more than my family lived on for a year when I was a kid.

I push my instinctive distrust of the wealthy aside and focus on Arun. The CCIA files said he was clean. My informants on Sally Ride confirmed his business is above board. That should have been enough.

Arun's contacts on Gagarin seemed a little shady, but anyone would say the same about my contacts on any given planet. And in an authoritarian nation like Gagarin, underworld connections could be valuable.

"I'm going to work from the assumption he didn't set us up." I load another of the flat breads with meat and veggies. Through the audio implant, I tell Elodie, "I don't trust him one hundred percent, but I'm not going to let Grigori know that."

She nods as she picks at her plate. "Do you have a plan for this… project?"

I hunch my shoulders, trying to look nervous and confused. "Grigori has a cover that will get me into the Imperial Palace. After that, I'm going to wing it."

"You're actually going to do it? Kill someone?" Her voice ratchets up.

I let my tone match hers. "What am I supposed to do? Let them kill you instead?"

Her eyes go wide, and she covers her face, sobbing. Through the implant, she asks, "How am I doing?"

I give her a tiny nod. "Don't over play it. And don't worry, I'll get us out of here."

Under the cover of even louder wailing, she winks. "I know."

SEVENTEEN

Two days later, we're still stuck on the moon base. Leo, Elodie, and I have breakfast with the crew each morning, and Elodie and I have had dinner in my cell each night. Our drones have mapped out the extent of the base including the location of the control room and the path back to the shuttle. I've done a couple more late-night recon missions, but I haven't seen Arun. He wasn't in his cell either time and didn't reply to my calls.

This morning, we eat the same meal as always—yogurt and fruit for me. Grigori consumes more pastry. I tasted a bit yesterday, but it was so sweet it made my teeth ache. I finish my tea.

Grigori rises, but I reach the door before him, blocking his way. "Where's Arun?"

Leo looks up from his meal. He's been very quiet every time I see him and hasn't responded to my attempts to call via audio implant. I can't tell if he's blocking my calls or something has been done to his device. During my nightly adventures, I haven't seen him. With his audio not responding, he could be sleeping in one of the many rooms I haven't had time to check. Arun could be there too, if they've done something similar to his implant. Or he could have deserted us.

Yleni moves to my side but doesn't touch me. She almost seems to be waiting for the answer.

"He's working on something for me." Grigori glares up at me. When we're both seated, it's easy to forget he's so tiny, but even standing, his short stature doesn't undermine his aura of authority. The attitude of Yleni and the other thugs make it clear he's not to be ignored or trifled with. "You'll see him when you accomplish your task."

He shifts to get around me, but I move with him, staying between him and the door. "Is he on the planet? Or here on the moon?"

"That's not really your concern. His location will not impact your mission. Which begins today. You'll take Arun's shuttle to the planet. My contacts have arranged a position for you as part of the staff at the Imperial Palace." His ability to arrange that makes me suspicious.

"A job at the palace? If you can get someone in so easily, why didn't you do that before? Why the eighteen massive attacks when a single assassin could be snuck in through the back door?"

"Seventeen. One of those wasn't mine." He shakes his head in mock dismay. "Didn't you study the information I gave you?"

I roll my eyes as loudly as I can. "Whatever. My question remains."

"My people are known. Their presence in the palace would be noticed." He presses his lips together as if this bothers him.

"You couldn't recruit anyone unknown?"

He flings out both arms. "I'm stuck here 350,000 klicks away. I can't just wander into a local pub and pick up a new crew."

"You sent a team to the station and grabbed Leo. Why weren't those people noticed?" I cross my arms. There are too many things he hasn't told me.

"We have friends on the station who… overlooked our little visit."

"Which is it, Greg?" I lean forward, forcing him to tilt his head back to maintain eye contact. "You have friends who can insert me into the Imperial staff, and friends who can cover up a kidnapping on the station, but you can't get one of your own people into the palace?"

He takes a step back and jerks his head at Yleni. "I don't need to explain myself to you. You answer to me. And your mission is today. Everything is in place."

"You want me to be successful, don't you?" I pull my arm away before Yleni can grab it. "I need as much information as—" My eyes dart to Leo, who's shaking his head slightly. "You *do* want me to succeed, right?"

Leo cringes and looks away.

Yleni takes a step closer, but her body is angled parallel to mine—almost as if she's allying herself with me. She takes my arm, but her grip is light. "Of course, he wants you to succeed. We all do. We want to return home!"

Grigori flings up both hands. "Listen to the woman! Why would I want you to fail?" He raises his voice, riling up his thugs. "We will rout the enemy! We will be victorious!"

Yleni cheers and yanks my arm, pulling me away from the door. "Do not doubt our cause! We will save our people and return to our planet!"

After Grigori leaves, Yleni drags me back to my cell. She flings the door open and shoves me inside. "Get your things. It is time to depart on your mission."

I move slowly, picking up the few things I've accumulated over the last three days—a tablet and stylus, since Grigori's computer system isn't compatible with my holo-ring. And I wouldn't have connected if I could—who knows what kind of spyware he would try to install on my system? I leave the teacup from last night's dinner on the table by the computer screen. When Yleni's focus switches to voices in the hallway, I slide my hand under the mattress to retrieve the knife I stole from the kitchen last night. It's too big to fit in any of my hidden pockets, but with only one guard, I should be able to keep it out of sight.

"What's Grigori up to today?"

She ignores the question. "Get moving, *postoronniy*. We have a schedule to keep."

"We do? What kind of schedule?"

"Landing times at the shuttle field were coordinated. Grigori had to pay off the officials, so we must land in the window they prescribed. In addition, his contacts at the palace have their own schedules."

I straighten the blanket on the cot. If timing is important, I can use that to my advantage. "How am I getting to the surface?" I tuck the knife flat against the underside of the tablet and let Yleni pull me down the corridor.

"I will fly you to the surface in your shuttle."

"My—you mean Arun's shuttle? You know how to fly it?" If Helva is still here, then where is Arun? He wouldn't have willingly left Helva behind, so he must be on the moon.

Or Grigori sent him somewhere. Maybe that's why I have to take Helva for my mission.

Thinking of Helva reassures me a little. Arun told us about her but didn't share that information with Grigori. Surely that proves he's not working with the little pirate.

Yleni glares at me. "It's a Commonwealth shuttle. A monkey can fly one."

"But can a monkey land it?" Actually, I know the answer to that question: yes. Most passenger shuttles are built with robust auto-pilot systems, and of course Helva could fly circles around any of those. Commonwealth law requires a human pilot in case of emergency, which is hilarious, since the automated systems generally do a much better job in crises.

"I don't know about a monkey, but I can land it." She pauses at the closed bulkhead doors. Through the thick glass, we can see a shuttle lifting off. The panels in the overhead split and slide aside, and the shuttle rises through the opening, then blasts away.

"Who was that?" I demand. Is Arun aboard that ship?

"Grigori took some of the men on another mission."

"What mission?"

She wrinkles her nose, her lips pressing together in disapproval of my question. Once the roof closes again, she presses her wrist device to the access panel. It beeps and the doors grind open. We pass through, and they begin closing immediately behind us.

"Elodie is a good pilot—maybe you should let her fly."

"I do not need a *postoronniy* pilot. I am fully trained to fly." She marches me across the landing pad and stops beside the shuttle. "Open the door."

I bite back a laugh. Fully trained but she can't get the door open. "I don't have access," I lie. "Arun and Elodie are the only ones who can open the door."

She glares at me. "I know this is not true. Open the door."

I lift both hands. "I'm just a security agent. I have no need to get into the shuttle without them."

"Arun has told Grigori you have access. Open the door."

"How are you going to fly if you can't even open the door?" I cross my arms and stare at her.

She grabs my wrist and yanks it away from my body, surprising me with her strength. Perhaps I have underestimated her abilities. She slaps my hand against the shuttle's access panel. "Shuttle, open!"

"That's not how—" The hatch pops, interrupting my denial. "Well, crap." I didn't open the app that allows access to the shuttle, which means the shuttle did this itself. Did Arun tell Helva to follow Yleni's instructions?

Whose side is he on?

EIGHTEEN

Yleni pushes me at the open hatch, slamming my shins into the edge of the airlock. "Get in."

"Hey!" I yank my arm away from her. "Get off me." I step into the shuttle. She pulls the door closed behind me and cycles the air. The inner hatch pops, and she pushes me toward it.

I stalk into the shuttle. Air circulates, blowing a chilly breeze against my neck. With no humans aboard, there was no need to keep it heated, but surely Helva didn't let Apawllo freeze? No, the space is chilly, but not cold.

"What's that?" Yleni sounds startled, but the finger she points is steady.

A pile of fabric on the right-side passenger seat moves, then Apawllo's flat face pushes free. His malevolent yellow eyes glare from between slitted lids, and he emits a sound halfway between a meow and a screech.

Yleni jerks back. "That is the ugliest cat I have ever seen."

"He's not ugly. He's got character." I'm surprised to hear myself defending the creature. Apawllo doesn't dislike me as much as he hates some people—"tolerates" is the word I'd use. That doesn't mean I'll let this outsider diss a member of my team.

Yleni skirts the cat as he stretches. Their expressions as they watch each other are hilariously similar. The cat leaps to the top of the co-pilot's backrest as the woman slides into the pilot's seat and orders, "Shuttle. Pre-flight."

"Preflight checklist onscreen." Helva's robot voice walks through the items, and checkmarks appear on the list as she describes the status of each.

I turn a little so Yleni can't see what I'm doing and flick my holo-ring.

"*Postoronniy*. Get up here. Sit there, where I can watch you." Yleni glares over her shoulder at me, pointing at the front right seat.

"Preflight check suspended," Helva says as the words flash across the checklist.

"No!" Yleni turns to wave a hand at the checklist. "Keep going."

The list slides aside in response to Yleni's swiping motion and disappears. "Preflight check terminated."

"Psst, Vanti." The soft voice in my ear sounds conspiratorial. "What's going on? Do you want me to play ball with this woman?"

"Restart preflight!" Yleni yells at the front window. "Why is it stopping?"

I saunter up the aisle and drop into the co-pilot's seat. "I dunno. I'm not a pilot. You need Elodie." Through my implant, I tell Helva. "Stall. We aren't leaving without Elodie."

"Got it." The checklist appears on screen again, but none of the items are checked off. Helva's mechanical-sounding voice says, "Pre-flight checklist onscreen." The list flashes, then scrolls down as a couple of items are added to the top. "Due to previous incorrect shutdown, the preflight system must reboot. All progress will be lost. Proceed?"

"What's the other option?" Yleni's hands flex as if she'd like to strangle the shuttle.

"Improper shutdown can lead to corrupted data, which could result in a poor navigational experience, incorrect calculation of fuel consumption, and possible death."

"Possible death?" Yleni's face goes pale, and her jaw clenches. "Reboot preflight system."

"Preflight system reboot confirmed. Estimated time, three minutes."

Yleni's fingers clench again, biting into the armrest. "Why does it take so long?"

I shrug. "This shuttle is temperamental. Elodie can make it behave, but I guess we'll just have to wait for the reboot."

Yleni looks at the countdown and grinds her teeth. "We should have plenty of time." She taps her fingers against the armrest in a nervous pattern.

"Draw it out, Helva," I whisper.

Something pings, and I take it as Helva's agreement. The lights dim, and the holo-screens go blank. Humming emanates from the speakers.

"What's the hold up?" a male voice cries from Yleni's wrist device.

She taps the screen. "Issue with the preflight check. The system is rebooting. Should take three minutes."

"Three minutes! That's crazy." The voice gets quiet, as if he's speaking to someone else. "Stupid *postoronniy* shuttles. Can you believe—"

Yleni cuts the transmission. "All of this automation bogs down your system. A Gagarian shuttle is much faster to start."

"Maybe we should take one of them instead." I peer through the windows, but there are no other craft in the landing bay. "Oh, wait. You don't have one."

"We have plenty of shuttles. They are in use."

"Doing something more important than the assassination attempt?"

Her eyes narrow. "Do not try to manipulate me, *postoronniy*. I have my orders, and I will carry them out."

"Whatever you say. We could get it done faster if Elodie was here, but I get it. You don't want a Commonwealth pilot showing you up."

"Your ridiculous attempts to injure my pride will not succeed. I do not need help."

Forty minutes later, sweat soaks Yleni's neckline and underarms. "Why will this shuttle not complete its preflight?"

I hide a smile. Helva has restarted the checklist seven times, adding longer reboot times and new items with each reboot. Currently, the top item, flashing red in time to an angry hooting, reads "re-initialize flux capacitor." I'm pretty sure I remember that name from one of the many ridiculous vids Elodie and Leo love.

"I hate to add pressure to your already stressful day—" My cheerful tone belies the sentiment as I point at the chrono display—the one part of the shuttle that has continued to work flawlessly. "But we aren't going to make our scheduled meeting."

Yleni grits her teeth and glares. At me, at the shuttle's dash, and finally at her wrist device. With an exasperated groan, she slaps her hand against the tiny screen. "Get that woman in here."

"The *postoronniy* woman?" the voice asks.

"No, I meant Diya. Yes, of course the *postoronniy* woman." She slaps the wrist screen again. "As if there is any other woman on this blasted—" Her comments devolve into muttered Gagarian that my translator simply identifies as, "assorted and inventive profanity."

A few minutes later, someone pounds on the side of the shuttle. The "airlock open" icon appears almost before Yleni swipes the command.

"Careful, Helva. Don't anticipate."

The shuttle sniffs disdainfully in my ear. "I didn't. Elodie opened the door."

The inner hatch opens, my ears popping with the slight change in pressure. Elodie steps inside and pauses. The cat launches himself from the back of the passenger seat, landing in her arms. "Wittle snooky-ookums, I've missed you so much!"

I suppress a snicker at the expression on Yleni's face—equal parts horror and contempt.

"Put that creature down and fix this shuttle." Yleni points at me, then flicks her finger to the seat behind the co-pilot's. "You. Move."

"Yes, ma'am." I take my time unfastening my seat restraints and moving to the passenger seat.

Once I'm settled, Elodie dumps Apawllo in my lap and slides into the co-pilot's chair. "What's the problem?"

Yleni waves at the pre-flight checklist just as the last item checks itself off. "This thing is—hey." She turns to glare at me. "What did you do?"

I lift both hands, holding them over the cat's back. "I haven't touched anything."

"It's working now—you can leave." Yleni glares at Elodie.

"But I just got here." She settles into the seat and reaches for the shoulder straps.

A stunner appears in Yleni's hand. "Get out. You aren't invited on this mission."

Elodie freezes, then slowly pushes the straps away from her body, keeping her hands visible. "I'm going." She lifts her hands above her shoulders as she turns her back, making a face at me.

I shrug and tell Helva, "Don't let her leave."

"Really?" Helva's sarcastic tone makes it clear she's offended by my orders. Like I should have trusted her to get it right. She doesn't know I don't trust anyone.

Elodie presses her ring against the panel beside the hatch, and it lights. The doors slide aside. Large words appear across the front shuttle window, red and flashing: "Airlock open. Launch sequence aborted." Helva's robot voice reads the statement aloud, and the preflight checklist appears again, all of the items unfinished. The lines shuffle down the screen, and a new one appears at the top, flashing red and white: "Secure inner hatch."

"What?!" Yleni swipes the checklist away and paws at the interface. "I should not have to restart the whole checklist just because the hatch opened! What kind of—" More profanity follows. I kind of wish I understood Gagarian—I haven't heard her repeat a word yet. Impressive.

"It's a failsafe." Elodie stops, one hand holding the airlock hatch halfway open. "You know the Commonwealth is a nanny state."

"I have flown Commonwealth shuttles before." Spit flies from Yleni's lips, and she shakes with anger. "None of them have done this.

I don't know how you're doing it, but you need to stop. Now. Or I will —" She yanks the stunner from its holster again and leaps from her seat, swinging it at me, then Elodie, and back. She stops, the weapon aimed at Apawllo, and a cruel smile settles on her lips. "Fix it. Now. Or the cat is dead. He won't survive a full charge." She cranks up the setting on the device.

Elodie sucks in a gasp. "No!"

Yleni jerks her stunner at the cat. "Fix it."

NINETEEN

While Elodie closes the hatch, I contact the shuttle. "Helva. Can you incapacitate her?"

"I don't have internal weapons. And anything I cobble together is going to impact you and Elodie too. As well as the cat."

"Can you do something with the audio—something that can be counterbalanced through our audio implants?"

"Ooh, good idea. It will take a little research on human tolerances—got it. This is going to be loud, but it shouldn't cause permanent ear damage. I hope."

Before I can respond, a piercing noise blasts through the shuttle, and my head. The cat seizes, his claws stabbing into my legs. I let out a yelp but can't hear it over the noise Helva has created.

In the front seat, Yleni has gone rigid, her hands clamped to her ears. I turn, but Elodie has disappeared. Leaning into the aisle between the seats, I see her crouched by the airlock, her face screwed up in pain, her arms wrapped around her head.

I look forward again just in time to see Yleni slump over sideways. Blood drips from her nose.

"You got her!" I can't hear my own voice over the intense din, but it cuts out almost immediately. I launch myself out of the seat and fall over on my face.

"Sorry." Helva's voice is gentle in my ear. "That particular frequency affects muscles."

I sit up on the deck, rubbing my nose where it impacted the floor. "Thanks for the heads up. At least it seems to have worn off quickly."

"Yeah, but you might want to visit the med pod when we get back to the ship."

"Why is that?" I manage to get to my knees, then climb slowly to my feet. "Do you have any slip ties?"

"Sure. In the galley." The door to the tiny compartment slides aside.

Clutching the backs of the seats to aid my shaking legs, I stumble back to the galley. "What were you saying about the med pod?"

A human-sounding cough sounds through my implant. "The heart is a muscle."

I close my eyes for a second, then go back to searching the galley drawers. "Great. How much damage did you cause? And how soon will it affect us?"

"Third drawer on the right." She pops the drawer open, revealing an assortment of hardware not normally stored in a galley. I push the solder gun and circuit boards aside, grab the ties, and head to the front of the shuttle, passing Elodie who sits on the deck, breathing hard. "You should be fine. You're young and very healthy."

I stop and turn slowly, looking back at Elodie. "But?"

"You need to keep an eye on her. She's older, not as athletic, and carrying a bit of extra weight. I'm sorry. I didn't take long enough to research it thoroughly."

You think, Helva? You researched for like twenty nano-seconds. "We needed an immediate action." I stumble forward and grab Yleni's arms, yanking them behind her back. "Speaking of which, can you imitate her voice and launch us?"

"Already in progress." The mass of holograms filling the front of the shuttle disappear, revealing a holo of the front windows. Through the hologram, I can see the blast shields closed across the plasglas. In the vid, the deck of the landing bay is far below us. The shuttle tips up. My brain tries to reconcile the vid with the solid, untilted deck under my feet and gives up. I sway as purple sparkles flare around the nose of the ship, and we push through the atmospheric barrier. "The sparks aren't real, of course. That's just so you can see where we're at."

I grunt as I bend down to secure Yleni's legs. I consider moving her to the rear of the shuttle, but she's taller than me and solid muscle. I'd need Elodie's help. Which would be dangerous for Elodie. "You got any cargo bots? Or grav-lifters?"

"Grav-belts in the cabinet where we hid the weapons."

I smack my forehead. "Or I could use my own. Where is my mind today?"

"I just scrambled it with a multi-channel digital amplification." She sighs.

I take off my belt and fasten it around Yleni's lax body. "It worked, though. She is out." With a flick of my holo-ring, the belt rises, lifting Yleni's abdomen, her head and legs sagging on either side. I set the altitude at a meter and a half above the deck, then push her over the seat backs to the rear of the shuttle.

When I reach the back, I leave her hanging overhead while I crouch beside Elodie. "Can I help you to a seat?"

"What happened? I feel so weak."

"Helva says the sound might have impacted your nervous system." I'm not going to say anything about her heart—even with current medical abilities, the possibility of heart attack is still terrifying. I slide my hands under her armpits. "Ready? Three, two—"

"On one? Or were you going to say three, two, one, lift?" A tiny thread of Elodie's usual humor lurks behind the soft question.

"On one. Three, two, one." I push upright, pulling Elodie with me. She manages to get vertical almost without my help, and we maneuver into a passenger seat. "Helva, can you recline this?"

The seat shifts, the back hinging down and the leg rest coming up. Through my implant, Helva tells me where to find blankets. "And your guest is waking up."

"Guest." I look up.

Yleni hangs from my grav-belt, her bound hands pulling her shoulders to an uncomfortable angle. She raises her head groggily, and her eyes flutter open.

"Good morning." I push her leg, setting her spinning. "Oops." A quick jerk stops her rotation, and I shove her toward the back of the ship.

"How did you—?" The words come out sloppily, as if her mouth isn't working properly. "What—"

"Don't bother. I'm not going to answer." I tap the holo-ring interface, and the grav-belt plummets. It catches her just before her head hits the deck, then descends gently the last few centimeters. "Nicer than you would have been to me."

She jack-knifes her body as I lean down to unfasten the belt, pushing herself across the deck more efficiently than I expected. She regained control of her muscles fast. I flick my holo-ring, and the belt yanks her up from the deck again, forcing an "oof" from her.

"I can leave you hanging here, but I want my belt back." I stalk closer.

She convulses her body, but I've set the belt to stationary, so she just flails in place. Gagarian curses flow out of her mouth, but since my app refuses to translate them, I ignore her. I send the belt to the center of the cargo hold, then use the controls by the rear ramp to lower a cargo net. Looping it beneath and around her, I secure the edges to rings in the overhead. The panel by the door allows me to tighten the netting, lashing her to the ceiling.

I'm not tall enough to reach her from here. I toggle my audio implant. "Helva? Where are the extra grav-belts?" Although our former captor is incapacitated, I don't want to give Yleni any more information than she already has.

Something clicks in the galley, and I move forward to peer inside. A hidden compartment has opened, revealing a quartet of high-end grav-belts. "Nice." I grab one and wrap it around my waist, pulling it tight. "Who did they make these for? They're huge."

"One size fits no one," Elodie mutters.

When I approach, Yleni begins struggling again. I decrease the elasticity of the net, which plasters her spread-eagle against the overhead. Rising in the borrowed grav-belt, I unfasten mine from her waist and work it free. Then I remove her wrist device. As I drop to the floor, she spits at me. I duck away with minimal splatter on my black jacket.

"Nice try. Good thing this is wipe-clean material." I swap out my belt, leaving the extra with Elodie. "You should stay here when we get to the planet but put this on—in case... whatever. It's always good to have a grav-belt."

She sits up slowly and takes the belt. "I want a shower and clean clothes more than a grav-belt."

"It will take a few hours to get to the planet at our current speed. The shower is all yours."

She grimaces. "Sonic shower. But that's better than nothing." As she carefully levers herself out of the chair, I pull her bright pink suitcase from the netting holding it to the deck and roll it to the door of the sanitation compartment.

While Elodie cleans up, I slouch in the co-pilot's chair. My audio implant pings with a private call from Helva. "Where are we going?"

I drum my fingers on the dash. "Back to the *Ostelah*, I guess. We need to formulate a plan to rescue Arun and Leo. I wish I'd figured out how to deactivate the tractor beam on that moon." I stare at the forward vid, trying to pick out the station, but it's too small against the brilliant colors of Gagarin.

"I might be able to help with that. But Arun isn't on the moon."

I jerk upright. "Where is he? And how do you know?"

"He snuck aboard Grigori's shuttle last night."

TWENTY

I POKE the shuttle dashboard to get Helva's attention. "Arun snuck aboard Grigori's shuttle? How did he do that? Where is it?"

Helva's smug voice still comes through my audio implant. "They launched shortly before you all showed up in the landing bay. He was still aboard."

"Did you talk to him?" I demand.

"I tried, but I couldn't connect."

I sag into the chair again swinging my legs up over the armrest. First Leo's comms were out, then Arun's. But Elodie and I have not had any problems. Did Grigori do something to the guys? "What tech could do that?"

"I've put together a list. It's longer than you'd expect." Helva throws a document up in front of me. It starts with accidental physical damage to the implant—from a fall or a blow to the head. I know from personal experience this is true, and Leo looked a little rough when we found him on the moon. But Arun hasn't been in any fights.

Or hadn't, last time I saw him. Who knows what he's been doing since then? The good news is he probably isn't in league with Grigori. If he was, he wouldn't need to sneak aboard the shuttle. I wish he'd contacted me before he did it. Of course, with his comms out—

I continue down the list. Intentional physical damage is next, along with a blood-chilling list of ways to accomplish that damage. Then a list of electronic means, including directed low-level electro-magnetic pulse or a stunner blast targeted to the right spot on the head. The list of possible cyber-attacks fills three full pages of scrolling. The final option—physical removal—has a footnote indicating the difficulty, recovery time necessary, and probability of irreparable damage to the owner.

"Yikes." I scroll up again, then back down. "This doesn't mention intentional deactivation by the bearer."

The list flickers, and that appears at the top. "I figured that was obvious." Helva's self-satisfied tone grates on my nerves.

She's a computer program, not a person. She—it *simulates human emotion. Get over it, Vanti.*

I swipe the list aside. It doesn't matter why his implant isn't working—there's no way for me to fix any of these remotely. "You said they left just ahead of us. Can you track them?"

"In progress. Their trajectory bypasses the station. They're headed for the planet." Helva throws a schematic in front of me with a dashed line showing their projected flight path. It arcs away from the station and around to the far side. "It's too early to tell, but it looks like they're headed for that smaller continent in the north. And based on their current vector, it looks like they're trying to land before the station comes over the horizon."

Unlike most stations in the Commonwealth, Leonov is not geostationary. It circles Gagarin in a Molniya orbit. I'm told the high-eccentricity and inclination make sense, since most of the habitable land on Gagarin is near the southern pole. Whatever the reason, the result is the station orbits the planet twice per day and doesn't hover over a set location. The Gagarians have comm and surveillance satellites, of course, so sneaking in under the radar is not really possible. Unless Grigori has done something to those satellites.

"Can you catch up to them? Close enough that we can follow them in."

"And not get caught by whatever surveillance they're avoiding?" Helva suggests cheerfully. "Sure. I can do that."

"We don't want them to see us, though."

"Really? I was going to scoot up on their butt and blast an air horn."

"Sarcasm is not your strong suit, Helva." Actually, that was pretty good, but I'm not telling her.

"I have analyzed centuries of situational comedies that would argue otherwise. But I forget your tiny human brain isn't capable of advanced reasoning."

Did she just call me stupid? I am going to rip her processor out of the shuttle with my bare hands if she doesn't back off. I take a deep breath. "Thanks." Luckily, I have years of experience hiding my true emotions. And implant comms aren't the most expressive anyway.

"Do I detect a hint of anger? I'm just joshing you, Vanti. Chill."

I grit my teeth. After I rip out her processor, I am going to melt it with my stunner, then jump up and down on it, then send it through the recycler. "What's our ETA?"

"Three hours and twenty-seven minutes."

"Good. I'm going to take a nap." I tilt my seat back. "Keep an eye on Elodie, will you? And our guest."

"I live to serve."

I don't try to hide the eye roll. I know she can see it.

I've just gotten comfortable when Yleni starts yelling. "Let me down from here!"

I open one eye, but I can't see her from this angle. "Shut up, or I'll tranq you."

"That would be better than hanging here wide awake!"

I flip a rude gesture over my head. I don't know if she can see it, but I don't care enough to look.

"I need to use the facilities."

"Don't care!"

"You will if I pee all over your cargo hold!"

"That's what cleaning bots are for." I pat down my pockets but can't find my ear plugs. I can turn on a noise-canceling routine, but then I might not hear Helva. Or Elodie, if she needs help. Heaving a heavy sigh, I get up.

Elodie emerges from the lav cubicle just before I reach it. Her face has more color, her hair—now green and pink stripes—is clean and fluffy, and she has a little bounce in her step. "Even a sonic shower can do wonders."

"You're feeling better, then?"

"A bit. Still tired." She rubs her breastbone. "And a little sore. Kind of all over, though."

I tap a panel on the outside of the cubicle. "System says your vital signs are good."

She turns to look at the display. "The bathroom has health monitoring in addition to the heated toilet seat? Fancy!"

"Arun buys the good stuff," Helva chirps.

"Who was that?" Yleni asks.

I close my eyes and reactivate my audio. "You couldn't keep quiet? I didn't want Yleni to know about you!" I turn slowly and say aloud. "The computer sounds really lifelike, doesn't it?"

Hanging from the ceiling, it's hard to gauge her expression, but I probably over-did the friendly tone. "That was the computer? I don't know why people like those realistic voices. I want my computer to sound like a computer."

I turn away and raise a brow at Elodie.

She shrugs infinitesimally. "I'm going to take a nap."

"Sounds good. We have another three hours until we land. I'm going to use the facilities and put on some clean clothes. Captivity stinks."

"You had a bed and a bathroom. I'm hanging from the ceiling!" Yleni squirms in her net.

"I didn't have a change of undies." I open my bag and pull out some clothing. "You can't wash 'em in the sink if you have nothing else to put on." I pause at the door to the bath pod. "You might want some earplugs. I think that one is going to keep grousing."

Elodie holds up a pink sleep mask with a ruffled edge and a little container with a SleepSound logo. "Got it covered."

"Hey!"

I shut the door, cutting off Yleni's complaint.

When I emerge later, clean and refreshed, the shuttle is dark. A line of faint green lights glow along the aisle between the seats, but the cargo hold is black. Soft, even breathing comes from both ends of the ship.

I activate a call to Helva. "What happened? Why is Yleni quiet?"

The shuttle laughs. "Elodie threatened her with the cat if she didn't shut up. Apparently, she's highly allergic. Don't worry, I'll keep an eye on her. Get some sleep."

"Thanks." I find a seat, recline it, and drift off.

"Rise and shine sleepy head!"

"Go away, Mom. I'm tired." I wave a hand in the direction the voice is coming from but touch nothing.

"I'm not your mother, and we'll be landing in about five minutes," Helva says. "Oh, and I took the liberty of downloading a full Gagarian-Standard translation data packet. You can add it to your holo-ring for off-line use."

"Thanks." Before my nap, I mentioned my problem using Grigori's computer. Helva came up with an answer and proactively implemented it. Maybe this AI thing isn't so bad.

I sit up, rubbing my eyes. The shuttle is still dim, lit only by the snow-covered landscape glowing beneath us through the front window. The planet turns slowly, the sun glittering along the far, curved edge. Helva must have the display set to low visibility—the glare should be painfully bright. "Where's Grigori?"

"He just landed." A red X appears superimposed over the planet, growing and shrinking slightly, so it appears to be breathing.

"Why's it going to take us five minutes to get there?" I get up—I need to do a few stretches to get my blood pumping again. It's been too long since I've had a decent workout.

The view changes, zooming out until the planet is fist-sized. "Because we aren't as close as that looked. I can shave a few seconds off, but I figured it will take them a while to arrange transportation, and you don't want them to see us land, right?"

"I keep forgetting that isn't an actual window. It looks so real. Bring up the lights, will you?" As I move to the cargo hold, the lights brighten. Yleni snores over my head. I avoid the damp spot I hope is drool and start a yoga routine. "Wake Elodie, please."

"Sure thing, boss. By the way, Arun's comms are back online."

I stand up so quickly my head spins. "Why didn't you say so! Did you contact him?"

For the first time, her voice sounds hesitant. "I wasn't sure that was a good idea. I mean, he's my owner—ugh, that feels so wrong—so slaver-ish to say!"

"You're a shuttle, Helva. Shuttles have owners."

"I don't *feel* like I should have an owner. I feel like I should be an independent person."

"Can we talk about AI freedom after we get out of this mess?"

"Fine. As I was saying, he's technically my owner, so I should get my instructions from him. But this whole 'taking people captive' thing really bugs me. And the kidnapping. I'm not sure I want to be associated with someone who thinks that's a good idea. If Arun is working with Grigori, or being controlled by him, then I'm not sure I should contact him."

I guess if my shuttle is going to have a moral crisis, I should be grateful she thinks I'm on the side of justice and right. I'm not going to point out that we are currently holding Yleni hostage and probably could be accused of kidnapping her.

"On the other hand, we have our own captive," Helva goes on. "But they started it."

"Yes, they did. But you said Arun snuck aboard the shuttle. Do you have reason to think he might be working with Grigori?" Feeling a bit more limber, I skirt the puddle of drool again and find my boots near the lav cube.

"Noooo—" She draws the word out, as if she's not sure. "But that shuttle is small. He can't possibly have stayed hidden. I mean, where would he...? They have to know he's there. So the fact that his audio is now connecting makes me think it's something they did. Which means they would want us to connect with him."

"Has he tried to contact you?"

"Not yet."

"I guess that makes sense. They don't know we're here—they think we're on the far side of the planet, assassinating the secretary general." I glare up at Yleni, still snoring and drooling in her net. "I suppose I need to let her use the facilities."

"You want me to release her?" As she speaks, one of the hooks holding the net to the overhead breaks free.

Yleni yelps, and her eyes fly open. She looks around blearily, then begins struggling. "Are you trying to kill me?"

"A fall of four meters isn't going to kill you. Especially since we're at three-quarters gravity." I pull out my stunner and point it at the green-haired woman. "I'm going to let you down. Don't try anything. Shuttle, set gravity to one quarter."

"Gravity, one-quarter," Helva says aloud in her robot voice.

"Release the rear starboard cargo clip."

Helva releases the rear port clip instead. Yleni yells again. She swings slowly, now draped across the net which is tethered at two diagonal corners.

"Ready? I'm going to have her—it drop you."

Yleni's head swings up and she glares at me. "Her?"

I shrug. "It sounds like a her. What can I say—I like to anthropomorphize the computer. Shuttle, drop the front clip." I'm not giving Helva a chance to misunderstand my commands. I wouldn't put it past her to reveal her existence just to spite me.

As if in response to my thought, she releases the back clip instead, and Yleni drops slowly. She curls into a ball as she descends, then rolls toward me as soon as she hits the deck. I'm not new to this whole hostage-taking thing, so by the time she rolls to her feet, I'm hovering near the overhead, my weapon still pointed at her. "Nicely done. That's good mobility after three hours netted to the ceiling." I give the stunner a little jerk to the side. "You can use the facilities."

Yleni looks at the door a half meter from her position, then glances toward Elodie, still sleeping in the co-pilot's chair.

"I wouldn't." I wave the stunner again. "I can easily take you down before you can reach her. And at the current setting, a stun is going to result in you voiding your bladder. You don't want to spend the next few hours in wet pants."

Her lips press together, but she opens the lav door and disappears inside.

"I'll watch her," Helva says through the implant. "Elodie is waking, and I don't like her heart rhythm."

I move to the front of the ship. "I cleared the lav—there's nothing in there she can use against us. But keep it locked until I say otherwise, okay?"

"You got it." Helva hums softly, the sound gradually fading out as if she's making her way aft.

Shaking my head, I place a hand on Elodie's shoulder. "How are you feeling?"

She groans and opens her eyes. "Like a truck ran me over. What the heck did Helva do?"

"Sh." I glance over my shoulder, but Yleni is still in the lav. "Don't say her name out loud. Yleni still thinks she's just a computer-run ship. Don't give her any ideas."

Elodie nods and sticks a thumb up. "Where are we? And what are you planning to do?"

"What I do best—improvise." I flick a hand at the screen, where our route is now displayed. "Grigori has landed. I'm going to assume Arun has been discovered—he snuck onto their shuttle. There's nowhere to hide. I'm going to have"—I glance behind me and lower my voice—"Helva drop me nearby, then take you back to the ship. I'll take Yleni with me—safer than leaving her here."

"I can handle a hostage!" Elodie laughs. "Words I never thought I'd say!"

"Normally, I'd agree. But you aren't well, and she's crafty. Plus, I don't want her anywhere near the *Ostelah*. And having my own hostage might be useful if we need to do a trade." I don't tell her I'll probably stun Yleni and stash her in a closet. "Does this shuttle have a survival cube?"

What? It's desolate out there, and I'm not a monster. Plus *I* might need it.

TWENTY-ONE

I PUSH the survival cube out over the icy ground. We've landed on the edge of a vast, snow-covered plain in front of a short cliff. Tall, jagged mountains rise above and beyond the stony wall. Grigori's shuttle landed at a base a few klicks to the east, two ridges past our current location.

My feet crunch and squeak in the pristine white covering—it's untouched, but not deep. I tuck the cube against the rocky bluff, under a narrow overhang. This survival cube expands into a single-room shelter. I open the panel, connect it to my holo-ring, and move back a few meters. Then I press "start."

The cube opens, the top rising and the walls folding out to create a larger cube, two meters on a side. When the whirring stops, I set the color scheme to white, and the walls mottle to a texture that blends in with the snowy environment. Anyone walking nearby would see it, but they'd also notice the grooves the shuttle's landing pads pressed into the snow. From a distance, the cube will be almost invisible.

I deactivate the homing beacon, so our new neighbors won't come to investigate, then check the latch on the door. The cube doesn't lock, but since Yleni could easily punch through a wall and escape, I don't care. But I set the latch to respond to my holo-ring to keep wildlife out.

Using my grav-belt, I swoop back into the shuttle. The survival cube comes pre-loaded with dehydrated food, but I don't plan on spending any time here. I load up a backpack with a couple more meal pacs and a water bottle with a built-in filter, then adjust the camouflage on my clothing to "snowy camo."

"Are you sure you want to take her?" Elodie tips her head toward the lav where Yleni is still sequestered. "We could leave her in there until you get back."

I activate a call to Elodie. "I don't trust her with Helva. The shuttle's AI seems to have a lot of discretionary decision-making built in. She—I mean *it* could decide Yleni should be in charge." I tell her about Arun's comms, and Helva choosing not to contact him.

Elodie hums in agreement. "Right. We can wait here and swoop in to save you."

I shake my head. "I want you back at the *Ostelah* and in a med-pod asap."

"Aw, I didn't know you cared so much, Vanti." She flings her arms around me.

I let the hug go on for a few seconds, then pull back. "Don't flatter yourself. You're my cover story. I need you."

She lets me go, still beaming. "Sure. You keep telling yourself that."

A flash of black streaks past us, making for the open rear airlock—Apawllo.

"No! Apawllo, come back!" Elodie rushes toward the opening but almost immediately stops, clutching her chest and breathing hard.

"Get strapped in." I shove her toward the front of the shuttle, then pound on the door to the sanitation cubicle. "Helva, open the lav."

"But Apawllo!"

"I'll get him."

The lav door slides open, and Yleni glares at me, her arms crossed. "Can't a girl have any privacy?"

"You've been in there for almost an hour. I figured you'd be ready to leave." I jerk my stunner at her. "Move."

She looks around the shuttle, then stalks toward the rear. At the end of the ramp, she stops, staring at the snow. "I don't have my winter gear." She lifts a foot to display her dark, low-topped shoes.

Wiggling my toes inside my sturdy but flexible boots, I shrug. "I guess you should be more prepared when you're taking someone on a suicide mission."

"I was supposed to drop you off. In Petrograd, where it's summer. Not frolic in the snow."

I wave the stunner at the survival cubicle. "Not my problem. Move."

She looks at the temporary building, then back at me. "What's the plan?"

"You're staying here. I'm doing something else. That's all you need to know. And I'll know if you leave the shelter, so don't. Except to—" I jerk my head back at the lav.

"Did you at least give me a shovel? So I can dig a latrine?"

"If I'm gone long enough that you need a latrine, you've got bigger problems."

"You're going to abandon me out here?"

"It's what you would do." I don't tell her I have set an automated alert to go to the local search and rescue if I don't return or reset it within ten hours. As I said, I'm not a monster. "I could just kill you." I holster my stunner and pull out my mini-blaster. "That would be much easier and waste fewer resources."

She smirks. "*That's* what I would do."

"Lovely. Get in the cube." I push the blaster muzzle at the building again.

She sighs, then trudges into the snow. I float behind her, safely out of reach. When she reaches the door, she turns before opening it. "I can help you."

"I don't need the kind of help you're offering." I drift closer.

She rubs her left wrist. "Can I at least have my *chet* back?"

I pull up my sleeve and wave the comm device at her. "You mean this? No, I might need it."

She glares at me. "It won't work for you. You don't know my passcodes."

I tap the screen and pull up a file with a grin. "I cracked your passcodes while you were in the lav."

She grinds her teeth. "It'll stop working—" She breaks off and presses her lips together.

"It might. But until then, it's mine." I move toward the cliff, keeping my weapon trained on Yleni, and call Helva. "Take Elodie home."

"Roger, boss." Helva's cheerful answer is almost drowned out by the clang of the airlock slamming shut. A few seconds later, the engines fire and the ship lifts away, the mild down-blast obscuring the impressions left by the landing gear.

Once they're airborne, I give Yleni a little finger wave. "I suggest you get inside and out of those wet shoes. Good luck."

She throws one more angry glare over her shoulder, then disappears into the cube.

I set a drone to circle the location, alerting me to any human activity, then lift away. Rising in front of the stony cliff, I look around but don't spot the cat. He's smart enough to come back to the cube when he gets hungry.

I hope.

Not that I care about the cat. But Elodie does, and I don't want her to get upset if he goes missing.

I reach the top of the rocky cliff and spot the little demon prowling along the flat top. His black fur makes him exceptionally easy to pick out against the snow. Which means he's probably going to get eaten before I get back. With a heavy sigh, I swoop down and land beside him. Crouching, I hold out both hands. "Come here."

The cat gives me his patented yellow glare, then stalks forward. He looks away but allows me to lift him. "I'm taking you to Yleni. Hopefully she won't eat you." She has a dozen meal pacs, so why would she? But I wouldn't put it past her to try to harm the thing in revenge.

Can I leave him to fend for himself? Probably. But do I want to deal with Elodie if he doesn't survive? Definitely not. And I don't want to explain that I left him in the charge of our ex-captor. I set him down and pull off my backpack. Rearranging the contents, I hold the open mouth toward him. "Your carriage awaits."

The cat gives me one more stink-eyed look, then steps daintily into the bag and curls up on top of the multi-tarp, closing his eyes. Mentally calling myself every stupid name in the book, I fasten the top and shrug the bag back onto my shoulders. He weighs a ton.

"Don't make me regret this."

The cat doesn't reply.

TWENTY-TWO

I LIE on my belly on a snowy ridge overlooking the "camp" where Grigori landed. "This place is pretty swanky for a rebel camp."

Apawllo doesn't answer, of course. I'm not sure why I'm talking to him—I've been a solo agent for many years. I don't need a partner to bounce my plans off. But for some reason, whispering to the cat seems to be helping me develop my strategy. Have I gotten soft?

The cat in my bag would imply I have.

I adjust my ocular lens to zoom in on the facility. Three large buildings, all painted a mottled white and pale gray—very similar to my clothing, in fact—sit at three corners of a rectangle. The fourth corner is a landing pad. Cleared paths run between, the faint red signature overlaid by my oc-lens indicating heated walkways. A lone tired tree droops under its load of snow in the center of the quadrangle. Grigori's shuttle sits on the otherwise empty pad—also free from snow despite the flakes currently drifting down. Heat from reentry takes a while to dissipate, and they've only been here an hour.

Someone exits one of the buildings, and I zoom in on him. Tall, with a turban and robe—it looks like Leo. But only from a distance. Up close, it's clear this is some other Leweian. Or someone dressed like a Leweian. Which makes me wonder, not for the first time, for why Leo—who has supposedly been in hiding for the last decade—wears Leweian clothing. I'll figure that out later.

"I'm going to call Arun." Ignoring the cat's silence, I put a call through my system. I'm close enough that I should be able to connect with him directly—if he's receiving.

A click tells me the call has gone through. "Arun?"

"Vanti?" Arun's voice is soft—he's obviously not speaking aloud.

"Sit rep."

After a brief pause, during which I wonder whether he understands my shorthand for "what heck is going on?" he sighs. "They got me."

"Acknowledged. What's your physical status?"

"Bruised. Possible broken ribs. Right eye is swollen shut. Left is not far behind."

"Can you see?"

"Barely. I'm in a cell on the third floor."

"Third floor? You mean third above the ground floor, or—"

A ghost of a laugh reassures me more than anything he's said so far. "Sally Ride third floor. We came up two sets of stairs."

I run a locator, and my system indicates his probable location on the building below. "Guards?"

He grunts a little, as if he's unsuccessfully trying to ignore the pain. "Two guys brought me up here, but it sounded like they left."

I shrug off the backpack, ignoring the cat as I dig out a pair of my insectile flying cams. Apawllo purrs, as if I'm petting him rather than shoving him out of the way. I program the drones to find a way into the building and launch them. "I'm checking. How'd they disable your audio implant? And how'd you get it back online?"

"They didn't disable it." He chuckles again, then groans. "They used a tinfoil hat."

A "tinfoil hat" is a device—often built into a helmet or head gear—that suppresses comm signals. It's the easiest way to isolate someone with an audio implant without damaging them or the equipment. Although if Arun has two black eyes, they weren't too worried about damage. They must intend to use his comm system later. "How do you know about tinfoil hats? And why'd they take it off?"

"I keep up on tech—even the supposedly secret tech. And have you looked around out there? The only person who would be looking for me is you, and they assured me you were busy on the other side of the planet assassinating Salahnovich. How's that going, by the way?"

I snicker. "That mission is on hold. Any idea how many people are in this place?"

"There were lots of people when we arrived. They didn't give me a tour, but the buildings seem to be in normal use. Folks wandering up and down the halls, sitting behind desks, nobody working too hard. You know, standard government employment."

"This is a government facility?" I stop scanning the area and focus on the doorway nearest me, zooming in to the extent my oc-lens allows. The data I downloaded from Helva allows my translator to decipher the Gagarian text: Yussupova Northern Base.

Zark. Yussupova is a huge research base. But "northern" must indicate this is a satellite facility because the actual Yussupova is close to Petrograd. "Are you saying Grigori landed on a government research base and walked in with a prisoner?"

The little huff of breath acknowledges the question. "Two prisoners."

"Who's the other one?"

"Leo, of course."

"Helva didn't say Leo was on the shuttle."

"Is she with you?"

I blink to return the oc-lens to standard focus, scanning the base again. Still no external activity. I guess the Gagarians here are indoor people. "You realize Helva is a shuttle, right? Where would I be hiding her?"

"I dunno. I'm not clear where you are."

"I'm on the ridge overlooking the base. About two klicks from you. Is Leo locked up too?"

"Yeah. I think they're planning on trading him for someone. When they caught me on the shuttle, I became a bonus."

"I guess I'll have to get you out before that happens. Who are they trading with?"

"If I had to guess, I'd say the Leweians, but they declined to offer that information. Leo looked nervous." His tone is tight and clipped, as if talking—even silently—hurts.

"Did he betray us? To Grigori?"

"I don't think so. From what little I overheard, I'd guess Grigori's gangs patrol the station, and they got lucky when they found Leo. Somehow, they knew about you and decided to rope you into doing the assassination."

Would Grigori really share his intentions with random underlings? I have my doubts about that, but I'm not going to voice them to Arun. They have him in custody—anything I tell him could be gotten out of him with enough time. "Any idea where Grigori and his goons are now? And how many of them he has?"

"He's got four with him. They appear to have free run of the base—at least, they had no problem landing and walking right in."

I crawl to a stunted pine tree for cover and get to my feet. The cat shifts in my bag, hissing a little. "I'm going to get you out."

"What about Leo?"

"Him too." I pull up a local file and check the location of the space station. It's beyond the horizon right now but will come into view in the next hour. Helva doesn't respond when I send a signal—based on the time passed, she should be docked there right now. "Hang on for a few more minutes."

"I'm not going anywhere without you."

I smile a little. "Can you fly Grigori's shuttle?"

"What about Helva?"

"She should be back soon, but taking his might be faster."

"I'm sure I could figure it out, but it won't be fast. I don't read Gagarian."

"You should probably work on that if you plan to continue doing business here."

His dry laugh holds zero humor. "Yeah, I'm not sure that's in the cards after this adventure. If the government sanctions kidnapping…"

"The GIDK do it all the time. In fact, I'm starting to think—"

"What?"

I shake my head, even though he obviously can't see me. "Not going to speculate." My ring vibrates. "Hang on, my drone found an opening."

I pull up the view from the drone's cam. The green cast indicates a low-light environment. It appears to be traveling through a duct of some kind. It makes two turns, then dives toward a grate, popping out into a room. The screen flares as the internal systems adjust to the suddenly brighter light. Location information scrolls up the side, placing it on the second floor at the far end from Arun.

The screen resolves. We're in an electronics lab. Three, no four people hunch over tall benches, messing with bulky green cards covered with silver lines. No one speaks. I push the little drone to the center of the room, where it rotates slowly, taking in the white, windowless space. I don't see any weapons, so I send the drone to the door, hoping there's a gap big enough to exit through. Setting it to find its own way out, I flip to the other one, which is also traveling through an enclosed space.

A few seconds later, it pings, and the screen flares. Then it clears, revealing this drone must have traveled through the plumbing and exited into a restroom. Luckily, there was no one nearby when it flew out of the sink faucet. The drones are tiny, but a faucet filter screen popping off, followed by a flying electronic beetle, would be hard to miss.

Relieved to have avoided detection, I set this drone to find access to the hall and grab the backpack. It feels lighter as I swing it over my shoulder. A quick check inside reveals the reason—Apawllo is gone.

TWENTY-THREE

TIGHTENING the straps on the backpack, I check the snow around me for footprints. Nothing. The cat probably jumped into the tree I had sheltered under. I peer through the boughs, but he doesn't look back. Ignoring the sinking of my stomach, I activate my grav-belt and drift down over the ridge, moving slowly so my camouflage has time to adjust to my surroundings. The tech makes me virtually invisible if I move carefully.

Slow and steady until I reach the cover of a shorter ridge, then I put on a burst of speed and charge forward. Cresting the lower hill, I drop my speed again.

That's when I spot the cat. He saunters along one of the base's heat-cleared paths as if he owns the place. I mentally shake my head in amazement—for a cat of his size, Apawllo can move crazy fast.

My slow drift finally takes me to the ground outside the compound, and I step into the shadow of a boulder to pull up the drone cams again. Location data indicates they've both made their way to the third floor. My breath catches in my throat. One hovers in front of a man whose swollen face is almost unrecognizable: Arun. A smear of crusty red covers the right side of his forehead and temple, with a couple of trails running down his cheek. His hair sticks up in all directions, dried blood stiffening the strands. His clothing is torn in several places, and he has no shoes.

I guess that's one way to secure a prisoner in the frozen wastes. I should have taken Yleni's.

I mark his location on my map, then turn to the other vid. This drone appears to be on the floor, looking up. Leo sits on a metal bench, cold sunlight pouring in from the window above his head. Grigori stares down at him, with two more standing behind, almost at attention. They each wear a blaster on their hips and the closer one holds a stunner in his hand.

I turn on the sound.

"…if you'd just tell us what we need to know. You don't owe him any loyalty." Grigori's soft voice sounds conversational, not threatening. He spreads his hands. "You left Lewei long ago. Why do you care who runs the place?"

Leo crosses his arms. He hasn't been harmed that I can see—his face is unmarked, and his turban and robe are clean and whole. He leans against the dingy gray wall staring up at Grigori without speaking.

I check the comms, but he's not appearing in my system. He could have a dozen tinfoil hats hidden inside his head covering. The devices aren't actually hats—just an apparatus that fits over the ear and physically covers the implant behind it. Easy to spot—unless the wearer is also sporting a hat. Or in this case, a turban.

Grigori shakes his head, as if Leo's silence troubles him greatly, then turns to face his guards. Leo lunges off the cot, getting an arm around the short man's neck in a move so fast it boggles my mind. I know Leo is fit, and that he practices several different martial arts, but moves like that are usually left to me.

He stands, his arms bulging as he lifts Grigori off the ground. The little man flails, kicking and swinging, his mouth working silently. Leo bats his hands away and ignores his kicks, apparently unperturbed by his prisoner's writhing. Grigori's eyes go big, and his hands grasp Leo's forearm as his face turns red.

"I suggest you drop those weapons." Leo's calm command snaps me into action. He's going to need backup. I lift off and speed toward the facility.

"Arun." I swipe the feed aside and rise up the side of the building, staying as close to the wall as I can. "Leo's taking matters into his own hands. Be ready to move."

"Got it. I don't have a holo-ring or grav-belt. Or anything."

"Who do you think is rescuing you? I've got it covered." I skim across the top of the building until I reach a spot above the hall outside his cell. "You might want to cower against the outer wall."

"Which one? There's no window in here."

Watching the screen, I direct him toward the outer wall, where he crouches in a corner. I land the drone on his shoulder, facing the door, then drop closer. My super-secret spy apps analyze the building. The roof is engineered to handle a heavy snow load but wasn't designed to prevent infiltration by a determined CCIA operative.

I dial the blaster powerpack to full and use my holo-ring to activate an off-label self-destruct sequence. "Fire in the hole."

I watch the drone footage, now showing me the door to Arun's cell, with a count-down on the side. Just as it ticks from seventeen to sixteen, the door opens.

"No!" Arun and I yell in chorus.

Leo stands in the hallway outside the cell, Grigori clutched to his chest. The little man stands on his toes, hands scrabbling at Leo's arm, neck stretched full length. Leo holds a blaster pointed at his captive's head. "Arun, come on."

"Get him inside and shut the door. NOW!" I scream. The clock ticks down. Ten. Nine.

Arun leaps up, the drone falling from his shoulder so I can't see what's happening. The audio gives me a confusion of yelling, thudding, and thumping. Then my countdown hits zero and the powerpack explodes.

The key to using the self-destruct on a blaster is placing it so the overload provides a useful detonation. Most people don't know there's a way to shape the charge—

"Arun! Report!" I slap a filter on my incoming audio to clear the static as I swoop toward the gaping hole in the roof. The uproar diminishes, but I still can't hear anything useful. "What happened? Are you okay?"

The vid is out; the drone has stopped transmitting. It probably got trampled. Or melted. I dive head-first through the smoking ruins of the building's roof, then pull into a fetal position to rotate and land on my feet in the rubble-strewn hall. The two goons from Leo's cell lay on the floor a few meters away, singed and smoking, but alive according to the triage overlay on my oc-lens.

I spin to face the cell. The door sags from melted hinges, hanging at an angle. Debris litters the floor, and flames lick up the wall. Smoke chokes me, and I pull my collar up over my nose and mouth, tightening the top edge of the built in mask against my skin. "Arun! Leo!"

The two men stagger through the smoke, dragging Grigori between them. The little man sags on his knees, his head drooping.

I unsnap the grav-belts from my backpack strap and toss them at Arun. "Put these on."

Arun fumbles the catch, then groans as he leans down to snag the belts. "What about him?"

"What about him? We aren't taking him with us." I glare at Grigori. Smoke rises from his singed hair.

"He's our insurance." Leo waits until Arun takes Grigori's arm before releasing the other one and snapping his belt on. Once it's in place, he grabs Grigori again. "We're going to need him to get clear of this place."

I point at the hole over my head. "You think? Bring him if you want." Grav-belts are built to lift up to a hundred and fifty kilos. Leo's slender frame combined with Grigori's short stature should mean their maximum mass is below the threshold. I rise through the smoldering hole to the roof.

A quartet of armed guards stand evenly spaced around my hole. I slowly lift my weapon-free hands, grimacing. "Don't shoot. We have your boss, and he's not going—"

The soldier on my left fires a blaster shot across the gaping hole, narrowly missing me. He yells something I can't understand. Is my translator broken? "Hey, dirtbag, I'm surrendering! Stop shooting!"

The same man yells back at me. This time, I recognize a couple of the curse words. My translator is definitely on the fritz.

Praying my communications are still active, I tell Arun, "They're up here. Head to the end of the building. I'll draw them off."

"We won't leave—"

"Don't be stupid. I'm trained for this. Do as I say, and we'll all get out alive. MOVE!" I slowly lower a hand toward my belt controls, watching the trigger-happy guy carefully as I continue ascending. "I'm going to come down now," I say loudly and slowly, pointing toward the roof. "Down." Fingers spread wide, I gently tap a single finger to my grav-belt controls.

My pre-programmed jump sequence launches me upward not quite as fast as the belt can go. I save that for real emergencies. But my belt is CCIA special issue, so it's fast. The Gagarian swear words are lost in the rush of air past my ears, but I imagine they're loud and fluent.

I look down without moving my head. At this velocity, any change in my posture would jackknife me into a hips-first position—literally flying by the seat of my pants. All four guards have abandoned the gaping hole and launched themselves after me. I let a tiny smile twist my lips. There's no way they'll catch me. Unless I let them. I want to give the others time to get away. I tap my grav-belt controls, and my upward trajectory stops with a head-wrenching jerk.

Hitting the down button sends me plummeting toward my pursuers at eye-watering speed. After a brief, disbelieving second, they scatter. Their terrified expressions make me laugh. I adjust my altitude and shoot away from the base toward the ridge I crossed earlier. "Arun, where are you?"

"We're heading down the stairs nearest my cell. We've still got Grigori, in case anyone tries to stop us."

"I'm not sure anyone will. There doesn't appear to be a lot of security here. I think they relied on stealth." Something isn't right about this place. According to my CCIA mission briefing, Gagarian research centers have some of the toughest security in the galaxy. But those four guards weren't wearing uniforms. I whip over the ridge, then around a tree, and stop, hiding behind its twisted trunk. My clothing automatically shifts to blend with the snow-covered boughs.

The four goons blunder on, still headed away from the base. I flip my oc-lens magnification to zoom in. They're Grigori's men, not Gagarian soldiers. As I watch, one of them peels away and pelts back toward the base. Probably just realized his boss is unprotected.

"Arun, sit rep!" I wait until the returning goon has gone over the ridge, then follow, giving him plenty of lead time. Then I dive down the icy hill, skimming a meter above the snow, trusting my enemy's haste to help hide me. At that speed, a quick glance over his shoulder isn't going to catch me. And if it does? I'll deal with that when it happens.

"We've reached the ground floor, and we're making our way toward the shuttle pad." Arun's response is jerky, as if he's out of breath or nervous. My system locks onto Arun's transmission, and a locator appears in my field of vision, streaking just above the cleared path toward the shuttle pad.

When this is over, I need to train Arun in evasive grav-belt maneuvers.

"Great. Get inside that shuttle and get it started if you can." I doubt they'll be able to do either, but that should keep Arun and Leo away from the goons until Helva returns. I toggle my comms and try to connect to our ship, but there's no response.

Ahead of me, the single guard jerks to the right, heading straight toward the shuttle pad.

So much for that idea. I increase my speed and altitude, closing in quickly. "Take cover," I tell Arun. "Bogie at two o'clock."

Still holding Grigori, Arun and Leo pause, then streak across the snow toward the closest building. This motion catches the attention of the guard, who swings left to intercept.

I put on a burst of speed and pull my stunner. With the grav-belt keeping my altitude steady, hitting the goon is easier than ordering a meal from an AutoKich'n. The beam hits him squarely in the back, and he sags. He must have been using manual controls on his belt because he plummets toward the snow-covered quad. The belt's emergency system halts his fall a meter above the ground, then dumps him in a heap.

I slide to a halt beside Arun and Leo. Grigori droops over Leo's shoulder, his head bouncing against the taller man's back. I point toward the landing pad. "Shuttle. Now."

We rocket forward, snow flying in a rooster tail in our wake. A quick check toward the hills reveals no goons returning. Reaching the shuttle, we drop to the tarmac near the passenger hatch. Apawllo sits beside the ramp, licking a paw. I stare at the cat for a second, then shake my head. I'm not going to question the abilities of the demon cat.

"Can you get this thing open?" I tap the shuttle's stubby winglet.

Arun grunts, his attention focused on the access panel beside the hatch. He already has it open and is poking inside. "You got any tools? I kinda lost my equipment back on the moon."

I snort a laugh at his dry delivery and fish a tool set out of my pocket. "Here." Our hands touch as I hand him the kit, sending an electric thrill up my arm.

I shove my reaction down deep. *You're on a mission, Vanti. Focus!*

Arun doesn't even glance at me as he takes the case. Maybe he didn't feel it. "Thanks. This shouldn't be too hard." He opens the kit and pulls out a tool, then does something inside the panel. The hatch slides aside. "Everyone in!"

I scoop up the cat and gesture for Leo to precede me. "You bringing your friend?"

Leo dumps Grigori's inert body into the airlock. "He might come in handy."

"We can leave him on the station." Arun waits for us to get inside, then closes the external hatch.

"We aren't going to the station." Standing over Grigori's body, Leo stares at Arun, the stunner still in his hand.

Arun stares back at Leo, his hand hovering over the internal controls. "Where are we going?"

Leo jerks the weapon, telling Arun to keep working. "We're heading to Petrograd. She has a secretary general to assassinate."

TWENTY-FOUR

Thoughts ping around my brain so fast I can't pin any of them down. I had just convinced myself Leo was on our side. "Are you crazy?" I drop the cat and pull my stunner, diving aside as he spins to fire at me.

He shouldn't have missed at that range. Crouching in the corner of the airlock, I stare up at him, my free hand hovering near my gravbelt. In this confined space, my emergency jump will launch me straight at him, hard enough to knock the breath out of him, likely breaking some ribs. And if his head hits the bulkhead, a concussion. "What are you doing?"

His eyes flick away from me, toward Arun, then up at the overhead. He cocks his head and raises a brow. His fingers drum nervously. "Don't you trust me?"

"I don't trust anyone." The words feel cold, but they're true. Not trusting has kept me alive.

"You trust him." He sounds sad as he nods at Arun. "And you just met him."

"*He's* not pointing a weapon at me." I slowly rise, my stunner still targeting him. "And I don't really trust him. I only met him a few weeks ago."

"Months." Arun pokes something in the open control panel again. "We need to get moving if we aren't going to be captured again. I assume you don't want that, Leo, since you were attempting to break out when she arrived."

I frown at Leo. "He's right. Whose side are you on?"

"I'm on my side." At Leo's feet, Grigori moans, and his eyes flicker. "Perfect. Terrible timing, Grigori."

The little man starts to sit up. "Leo! What—"

I fire my stunner. Grigori flops to the floor, out cold again. Leo and Arun gape at me. "What? We don't need him mucking things up. We've got enough to sort out here. And despite what you think, I don't completely distrust you, Leo. I mean, I didn't, until this whole standoff thing. You must have a good reason—or at least what you think is a good reason—for wanting me to complete Grigori's mission. I want to know what it is."

"Whatever it is, it's going to have to wait." The inner hatch opens, and Arun closes the access panel. "Grigori still has three friends out there." He disappears into the craft.

Leo jerks the weapon, urging me to follow.

I suppress an eye roll. "You know I could take that away from you." Although remembering his attack on Grigori, maybe he wouldn't be as easy to take down as I think.

"Probably." He holsters the weapon and bows, waving one hand toward the open hatch with a flourish. "Please, my lady, after you."

This time, I let my eyes roll. Hard. "What's your plan?"

He looks at the overhead again, then wiggles his fingers toward the body of the shuttle.

"Hey, guys? We've got incoming." Arun's voice filters in through the opening.

Ignoring Leo, I lurch through the opening and hurry forward. This shuttle is larger than Helva, with two rows of two seats each behind the pilot and co-pilot's area. Across from the airlock, there's a galley, the lav, and another hatch leading to the large cargo hold. A pile of discarded clothing lies on the deck behind the seats on the right, and the air smells like sweaty socks.

Apawllo leaps to the back of one of the passenger seats and stretches across the top. I drop into the seat beside Arun. Leo takes the chair behind him, where he can maintain a clear view of me.

At least I assume that's why he chose that seat. It's what I would have done.

The front viewscreen shows three small figures flying about twenty meters above the ground, growing larger as they approach at top speed. Arun nods at them as his hands fly over the controls. "Your friends are here."

"How many guys did Grigori bring?" I ask Leo, searching the dash in front of me for anything resembling weapons. This shuttle is old tech. While the view screen appears to be a projection rather than an actual window, the controls are all physical buttons and switches. I flick my holo-ring and bring up my translator, then point at a button. "We've got flares."

"He had six. The two you took out in the hallway. The one you took down out there." Leo holds up his hands, left fingers and right thumb extended. He nods toward the buildings as he folds down both thumbs and the index finger, counting. "And those three." He points the last three fingers at the screen.

"And none already on site?" I slide a light finger across buttons on the dash, making mental notes of the comm system, life support, and —does that say music? "Will the locals try to help him?"

"Yes and no." Leo frowns, then shrugs. "Remember when Grigori told us most of his supporters had been relocated, and only the fighters were with him on Titov?"

I nod.

"This is where they were relocated to."

"I thought he said they were off planet." I peer at the screen, trying to spot anyone, but the place is desolate.

"He implied it. But there's a huge underground facility here, where most of the families are hiding. The 'researchers' are fakes—to keep the Gagarian government from investigating. From time to time, they send in reports on their recent failures. This government is so used to failure, no one questions them. And they've been lucky—the authorities haven't sent anyone in person." He laughs dryly. "It's not a popular destination."

"Got it." Arun presses his hand against the control surface as the shuttle hums to life. The lights flicker, then brighten, and a targeting screen appears over the forward view. Three rows of buttons on my side of the cockpit light. My system translates the labels to "laser," "pulse cannon," and "baster."

"Baster? Like for a turkey?" I poke at that one, and a beam lances out, frying the lone tree in the center of the quad. The guys flying toward us scatter. "Blaster! Cool."

Arun looks at the tree-turned-torch and closes his eyes for a second. "I'm glad all the good guys are inside." He flicks a few more buttons, and the shuttle vibrates, then lifts off.

I graciously ignore his snark. Using a trackball on the dash, I set targets on the three goons. If they have even rudimentary defensive systems, they should be notified when we lock on. Before I complete the thought, the three jerk away from their current trajectories, jinking and swooping in an effort to break free. I have no intention of firing, but it's fun to see them squirm.

"Who's that?" Arun points at the viewscreen, indicating a small figure sliding down the face of the ridge. It plows snow as it descends, leaving an obvious trail behind.

I use the targeting system to zoom in. A bristle of green hair confirms my suspicion. "That's Yleni. She made excellent time. Almost as fast as the cat."

Arun grunts but remains focused on his controls.

"The cat?" Leo asks.

I jut a thumb at Apawllo. "He got here on his own."

"Huh." He taps Arun on the shoulder. "Petrograd. Don't try any tricks."

Arun connects a call to me. "What's the plan?"

"I want to find out why he's so desperate to help Grigori." I flick my holo-ring and open my suite of hidden spyware. Pulling the screen large so Leo can see the app titles, I tap the one labeled "Silencer." The red holo flickers and turns green. I peer at Leo through the interface, his face looking sickly behind the colored icon. "That app cuts all comms. Even internal ones." I tap behind my ear.

Arun gives me a quick look but doesn't contradict me. Our point-to-point call is still active, but I want Leo to think he's safe. With the app running, no one can monitor us from outside the shuttle. And Grigori is out cold, so it's as safe as he's going to get. "Tell us what's really going on. Why do you want us to help Grigori?"

"They have Elodie."

TWENTY-FIVE

I shake my head at Leo. "No, they don't have Elodie. She's back on the *Ostelah*. She dropped me and Yleni here and flew back."

"Yes. And then they grabbed her." Leo's fingers twist in his lap. "Grigori showed me a vid."

"Where?"

"It was on his chet." Leo taps his bare wrist and flicks his gaze at Arun's back. "Raynaud—my engineer—is working with them."

Arun jerks, and the shuttle rumbles, making it hard to hear Leo's words. I open my mouth to tell Arun to dampen the sound, then realize he would if he could. Gagarian tech is decades behind the Commonwealth, and he's completely unfamiliar with this vehicle.

"We'll reach orbit in three minutes." A countdown appears on the screen. Arun slides his hand across the control surface, and the ride smooths a little. "This tub has no gravity, so strap in."

"I need to do something first. Can I open the airlock?" I push out of my seat and head aft.

"It's possible. Not advised in flight, but it won't damage anything."

"Perfect." I tap the access panel. "Check the cams, please."

After an audible click, he calls back. "Grigori is still out."

"Thanks." Whatever Arun did to the access panel allows me to open the hatch without security credentials—which is a good thing, since faking those would take time I don't have right now. I push the hatch aside, hanging back a moment to make sure Grigori wasn't faking for the cams. When he doesn't rush me, I move into the smaller space. Watching carefully, I pat down his pockets and locate two holo-rings, then pull his "chet" from his wrist.

Grabbing a cargo strap from the compartment near the hold, I return to the airlock and strap the little man to the deck. When he revives, he'll be able to unstrap himself easily, but he won't float around the airlock in the meantime.

I get back to the cockpit with ten seconds to spare. Yanking the straps across my shoulders, I click the ends into the buckle and tighten it as I start to drift above my seat. Then I hand the wrist device to Leo. "Can you access that vid?"

Surprise flashes in his eyes, then he takes the device. "You trust me not to call for help or override the shuttle?"

"Trust is a strong word. My suppression app will block any attempted calls. And I'm ninety-nine percent sure a person at the controls has priority over remote piloting." I wave a hand at Arun.

"Besides, we're locked into orbit now. Nothing you can do would change that." Arun pulls his hands from the controls and turns sideways in his seat to peer around the back at Leo. "I want to see this vid."

Leo nods and straps the device on his arm. While he works on it, I offer the two holo-rings to Arun. One is smooth and black, the other is silver with a carved surface, like a signet ring. "I assume one of these is yours?"

Arun takes the silver one, leaving the other in my palm. "I was afraid I'd never see this again." He slides it onto his finger, then flicks it to bring up the welcome screen. "Hello, old friend."

"That's why I use generic rings." I lift my hand, showing my smooth steel ring. "Although I'm glad Grigori didn't take them when we landed on Titov. It would have been impossible to replace here."

"Not impossible—just extremely expensive." Arun closes the holo. "A few places import them—that's what I was working with Dima on."

"I didn't know the Commonwealth was allowing that tech to be exported."

"It's getting here on the black market, so we lobbied for legal means to sell them." He rubs his finger and thumb together in the ancient sign for credits. "Everyone wants to make a little scratch."

"A little?" Leo looks up from the chet with a mirthless laugh. "The Gagarian government wants to make a lot of scratch. They have their fingers in every transaction—including your friend Dima's. And Grigori's. Here's the vid."

We crane our necks to see the tiny screen on Leo's arm. On it, a man whose features are blurred holds Elodie's arm. She looks terrible—her hair messy, her face streaked with tears, her skin pale. "Help me, Vanti! You're my only hope!"

I point at the screen. "That's code."

"What?" Leo looks up from the replay. "I recognize the quote, but I thought—"

"Not the quote." I shake my head. "I'm talking about her hands." I reach over and try to swipe the vid back. Nothing happens. "Replay it, will you?"

Leo does something to the screen, and it starts the vid again.

"Stop!" I point at the now frozen screen. "See her fingers? She's spelling out something. That's a C."

We step through the vid. Using the finger signals I taught her when we first started working together, she spells out "cam."

"Yes!" I laugh. "Can you zoom in? She must be wearing one of her hidden cams."

A ping and a voice speaking Gagarian bring Arun's attention back to the shuttle. "We need to decide where we're going."

"Not back to the ship." I twist around to face the front, using my restraints for leverage against freefall, then flip through my holo-ring to an interface with the *Ostelah*. "I need to be close enough to connect with the ship, but if Raynaud is really working with Grigori, we can't dock."

"I haven't seen any proof he's with Grigori." Arun's tone as he works the control surface again is flat and disbelieving.

Leo shuts down the vid. "Grigori told me. That's how he knew when I went into the ship's access lobby."

An inside job makes sense. I'm still not sure we can trust everything Leo says, but I know less about Raynaud than Leo. I should have run a more extensive background on him before I allowed Elodie to fly on the *Ostelah*. Instead, I let my feelings—my friendship—with Arun cloud my judgment. I trusted his vetting process when I *know* I can only trust my own.

"Okay, we're in a following orbit, behind the station." Arun throws a schematic on the screen, showing our position relative to the planet and the station. A little blue light blinks a few centimeters behind the larger green light indicating Leonov Station. "I've registered with the station, using the shuttle's credentials, claiming a malfunction that won't allow us to dock. They're sending a repair bot, but that will take hours."

"They think we're Grigori?" I ask.

"No. This shuttle is registered to someone named Nortov. Remember, Grigori is kind of in exile."

I nod, then look at Leo. "Is there any kind of med pod on this boat? Arun looks bad."

Arun smiles, showing off a split lip. "I'm okay. It's mostly superficial." He pokes a finger at his swollen eye and winces.

"No, you aren't okay. And if we have to rescue Elodie, we need you in good shape." I raise a brow at Leo.

"There should be a med wand in the first aid kit." Leo points toward the lav. "It won't do cosmetic stuff, but it should seal any cuts and bring down the swelling."

I turn back to Arun. "See if you can reach Helva without alerting Raynaud. And then head to the lav and use the med wand while I work out a plan."

While Arun complies, I flip through screens, checking vid feeds until I finally find an active one. "Ha! Got it." Nubby green fabric fills the view, with some plastek and a tiny sign that says something in Gagarian. I throw the vid up on the front screen.

Or at least I try, then I remember this shuttle doesn't have that tech. Grumbling under my breath, I stretch the holo as big as it will go. "This is the live feed from Elodie's cam. It looks like she's on a shuttle—maybe a commercial one?" I try to connect to her audio implant but get nothing. I flip to another app. "They must have put a tinfoil hat on her. I'm going to try to use this vid feed to locate—got it."

"Where is she?" Arun and Leo both lean toward me.

"Shuttle headed dirtside." I check the cam feed again. Now it shows one of Elodie's hands clutching a laminated card. I run the text through my translator and laugh. "That's the safety card for the Leonov to Petrograd shuttle! Excellent spycraft, Elodie! They land at Petrograd field in about twenty minutes. Can we catch them?"

Arun shakes his head but starts flipping switches and pushing buttons. "They've got too big a head start. But we can land at Bondarenko's and get ground transport there. Keep tracking her."

"Can we trust Bondarenko?" I swipe the cam feed to the side and connect the tracker to my mapping software.

"To let us park this shuttle, no questions asked for a huge fee? Yes. I'll get Dima to arrange ground transport. As far as trusting *him*—" Arun rocks his hand back and forth. "I trust him to get us safe ground transport and to keep our landing under his hat. I'm not giving him any details." He presses a button, and the shuttle jerks, movement pressing us into our seats as we dive toward the planet. Then he flicks his holo-ring and initiates a call.

Arun speaks to someone in what sounds like fluent Gagarian. I catch a few words, including Bondarenko, Dima, and Petrograd. While he chats, I troubleshoot my translator. Unfortunately, the process is fast and easy—data overload has corrupted the files.

By the time we land at Bondarenko's, Grigori is awake again. "What are we going to do about him?" I point at the airlock feed where the little man struggles to unlatch the cargo strap. He must have zero experience—they aren't that hard to open.

"If this was Helva, I'd have her dump him out in the countryside." Arun works through the shutdown checklist. "Like a captured rodent you don't want to kill."

"Who's Helva? That's the second time you've mentioned her." Leo unfastens his restraints.

Arun and I exchange a look. I forgot Leo hasn't traveled in Helva. I give a tiny head shake. The less Leo knows, the better.

"That's what I call my shuttle." Arun resumes his shut down procedures. "It has a really good programmable autopilot." He flexes his fingers as if programming.

I move toward the airlock. "Maybe we can program the *limuzin* to take him."

Arun flicks the last switch, and the controls go dark, including the view screen. "There's no *limuzin*. You and Elodie got the official government VIP treatment. We'll have an *autotaksi*. And I doubt they're programmable." He waits for me to open the airlock but puts an arm across the entrance when I get it open. "You wait here. Keep him under control." He nods at Grigori, still lying on the deck fumbling with the cargo strap latch.

I pull out my stunner, lean forward, and flick the strap catch. "Get up."

Grigori spits Gagarian at me as he climbs to his feet. Arun lurches forward and slaps his face. "You will not speak to a lady like that!"

The little man yelps. Red blossoms across his cheek, and he rubs it. "She's no lady."

Arun's hand swings back, but I grab his arm before he can slap Grigori again. "He's right. And I didn't understand it anyway." Turning so Grigori can't see my face, I point to my ear and mouth, "broken."

"Doesn't matter. That was vile." He shoves Grigori toward me. "Take him into cargo. I can get some spray adhesive from Bondarenko, so you can glue him to the deck if you want."

"Not necessary." I step back, so Grigori can move past me into the shuttle without coming within reach of my weapons. "You heard the man. Cargo."

He mutters under his breath but opens the rear hatch. I follow him in, then stop in amazement. "What is all of this?"

TWENTY-SIX

CRATES FILL the hold of Grigori's shuttle, leaving only a narrow aisle down the center. The stacks go nearly to the three-meter-high overhead.

I tap one of the boxes. "What's in these? Were you supposed to deliver them to that base?"

"Yes. This was for Yussupova base." Grigori purses his lips.

"And...?"

"And what? We didn't deliver it because you stole my shuttle!"

"Hey, you kidnapped my friends first, so I don't want to hear it." I glance at the closest stack of crates, but I can't read the Gagarian writing. I blink my oc-lens and open my translation program one-handed. The app is still on the fritz—I get nothing useful. "These look like insulated crates."

"They are. It's food." Grigori props his fists on his hips and glares at me.

"From Titov? Your hydroponics are that good?" I jerk the stunner up the stack of crates. "That's a lot. Doesn't your base get supplies from—" I break off as I realize two things. First—his base is a fake government installation on an isolated continent. They might get some supplies—since the government seems to think their research is real—but only enough for the "researchers" who are assigned there. And second—any supplies they get won't be nearly enough for the massive underground facility where Grigori's people—families, with children—live.

I glare at Grigori, wishing I'd never opened the cargo hold. I can't be responsible for hundreds of children starving. And there's no doubt in my mind they will if this shuttle full of food doesn't reach them.

But if I let Grigori go, he's going to either turn us in or demand we complete the assassination. He clearly doesn't have any qualms about abusing innocents. I'm starting to wish we'd kept Yleni. She, at least, seemed to have a conscience.

"Leo!" I call through the open hatch. "Grab some slip ties."

"On it." The sound of someone rummaging through drawers reaches my ears. "Ow! Zark!" Something slams closed. More rummaging. Then Leo appears in the opening, a wad of slip ties in one hand, the index finger of the other in his mouth. He offers the ties and removes the finger to say, "Who doesn't put a cover on a knife in a drawer? That would never fly at the Hopper-Child Institute."

I take the slip ties and hand the stunner to Leo. "Keep him covered." I step closer to the little man, staying out of Leo's line of sight, and make a twirling motion with my finger. "Turn around. Hands behind you." I fasten Grigori's hands behind his back and use another tie to secure his arms to one of the crates in the third row. He might be able to pull free, but not without a couple of boxes landing on his head.

Retrieving my weapon from Leo, I head back through the hatch. Behind me, Grigori utters a string of angry sounding words. Leo replies, then says in Standard, "Don't worry. We'll be back."

Leo closes the hatch with a whomp, and we move to the seats in the forward part of the cabin. I turn to face him. "I need to rescue Elodie, but there's enough food back there for—I dunno. A lot of people. If it's really food."

Leo nods. "It's food."

"How do you know?"

"I helped load it. Sneaked a peek in a couple of the crates. Might be other stuff stashed in there, but most of it is food." Leo sticks his finger in his mouth again.

I roll my eyes and pull a tiny dropper of elasto-seal from my pocket. "Just bandage that, will you?" While he takes care of his wound, I drum my fingers against the armrest, sorting out plans. "If we let Grigori have his shuttle back, what will he do? Will he take the food to his people or try to carry out his insane assassination?"

Leo snorts. "He's not going to do it himself. He knows it's got a ninety-eight percent chance of failure." His eyes cut to me, then back to his finger. "Eighty percent with you. That's why he grabbed us. You're his only hope."

"Enough with the *Ancient TēVē* already." I tap the back of his head with a gentle whack. "At least use a new quote."

"Ow." He drops the elasto-seal and rubs the base of his skull.

"That didn't hurt."

"Didn't hurt your hand. My head is sensitive."

"You have like forty layers of fabric in that turban. There's no way you felt that." I grab the little dropper from his knee and make sure the cap is secure before returning it to my pocket. "What's taking Arun so long?"

As if in response to my question, the airlock alert pings. The outer hatch opens, and the vid still onscreen shows Arun and Dima Sadiki entering the airlock. Arun looks up at the cam and his audio connects to mine. "Dima was here with Bondarenko. You got Grigori stashed in cargo?"

"Yup. It's all clear in here." I swipe vids down to thumbnails and flip through the shuttle cams to turn off the one in cargo. Then I activate the inner airlock. "Come inside."

Dima strolls in as if he owns the place, looking over the ship and nodding. "Nice. Sturdy. Solid build. Trade is possible." He peers into the lav, then steps into the tiny galley.

I raise a brow at Arun.

"I needed something tangible to swap." Arun's voice is soft through my implant.

"You offered a whole shuttle in exchange for a cab ride?"

"No, of course not. I told him we might be able to trade something. He asked what, and I said let's look aboard. You don't think he wants the whole ship?"

I close my eyes. How can someone as smart and business savvy as Arun be so dense? "That's exactly what it sounds like to me. He's not looking through the cabinets."

Arun spits out an expletive.

Dima steps out of the galley. "*Zark* is swear word?" He repeats the word a couple of times. "I like. I can see the hold?"

"We have some… temperature sensitive cargo." I jump out of my seat.

"Ah, beautiful Vanti!" Dima peers past me. "Where is lovely Elodie?" His gaze slides over Leo without obvious recognition.

"We're meeting Elodie in town. Hence the transport." Arun takes Dima's arm and moves him toward the hatch. "But I forgot about the cargo. We need to deliver that."

Dima's affable expression goes blank. "You 'forgot' your cargo? This is not—"

"It's mine." I lurch toward the men. "I asked Arun to transport some items for me. Perhaps I can arrange ground transportation for them." I can't, obviously, but he doesn't know that. I give Dima a coy smile.

His eyelids droop a little as he gives me a sleezy once-over. I clench my fists behind my back, so I don't wipe that creepy look off his face.

"Maybe I have interest in your cargo. Something worth a trade." He reaches toward me, as if to touch the lock of hair that has fallen from my ponytail.

Almost faster than I can think, my hand snaps out and I seize Dima's index finger in my fist, bending it backwards. In the same instance, Arun's hand falls on Dima's shoulder, spinning him away from me. Dima screams. Releasing my grip, I jump back. "Arun, no!"

Arun freezes, his elbow cocked, fist clenched, ready to pound

Dima's face. He glances at me, then drops the Gagarian, stepping back, hands raised. "Don't touch her."

A little thrill goes through me at the words, followed by a wash of dismay. I don't need him to protect me. But it feels good that he wants to.

Dima lifts both hands. "I did not know you are together." He bows, hands out to the sides. "I would not wish to come between a man and his—" I don't understand the last word, but combined with another smirking once-over, I get the sleezy idea.

"*Out!*" Arun shoves Dima toward the airlock. "Get out. We're done."

Dima frowns, his hands lowering. "I meant no disrespect."

"Sure you didn't. Get out of my shuttle. Now!"

The Gagarian smirks. "But it isn't your shuttle, is it? Perhaps I will place a call to the authorities and let them discover whose shuttle it is."

Arun yanks out his stunner as Dima pulls his own weapon. The two men stare at each other, breathing hard, jaws clenched, nostrils flaring. The similarity would be funny if our situation were less desperate.

"Now what?" Arun asks.

"Good question. My people will search if I go missing. Will anyone notice if *you* do?"

They glare at each other for a few more seconds.

"This is stupid." I pull my stunner and fire.

Dima drops to the deck.

"Vanti!" Arun stares at me, his weapon still aimed where Dima stood between us.

"Put that away." Ignoring his stunner, I yank the spare slip ties from my belt pouch and crouch to roll the prone man so I can secure his arms.

"What are we going to do with him?" Arun runs a hand through his thick hair, making it stand on end. "You can't go around stunning one of the most powerful men on the planet."

"Is that who he is?" I rise, gesturing at Dima. "I thought he was a *business associate*."

"He is. But his business is tightly entangled with the Gagarian government. That's what makes him so useful as a trade partner. I'm trying to set up more than just a small-time shipping deal."

I gesture at Dima. "Help me move him to cargo, will you?"

Arun leans over and lifts Dima's shoulders from the deck, dragging him toward the cargo hold. "Are you sure that's a good idea? He and Grigori might—" He shakes his head sharply. "I have no idea how they will react to each other."

I use my grav-belt to lift off the deck and over Dima's body, twisting around Arun to open the hatch to the cargo hold. "If Dima is in league with the government, he and Grigori are not on the same side. Probably. But we should still keep them apart." I hesitate in the open hatch. Maybe we should stash Dima in the lav instead.

Arun stops. "What's your plan?"

Good question. What is my plan?

TWENTY-SEVEN

I GET Leo to rearrange a few crates in the cargo hold, creating a niche out of Grigori's view. The little man asks incessant questions, like a five-year-old. I finally shut him up by threatening to stun him. While Leo escorts Grigori to the lav, we secure Dima in his new cubby, out of sight of the entry hatch. As I secure his hands, I tell Arun my new idea.

Arun rubs his forehead as if my plan causes him physical pain. "Are you sure it will work?"

I stare at him, then snap my jaw shut, remembering Arun and I haven't worked together for long. He isn't used to my improvisational style. "No, of course I'm not *sure* it will work. But there's a pretty good chance it will help us accomplish our goals."

"Help us accomplish our goals? That seems a bit more cagy than saying it will work."

I wave a hand. "It's a work in progress. Besides, a plan never survives first contact with the enemy."

"Is that a quote?"

"Yeah. Sun Tsu. Or maybe Kim Kardashian."

Leo and Grigori return. The little man stops in front of me, leaning against Leo's pull. "You gonna take out Salahnovich?"

"Why would I do that?"

"Because if you don't, my friends will kill your friend." His lips curl in an evil grin.

"What are you talking about?" I fake confusion, grabbing his arm and shaking it.

"Your friend, Elodie. My people have her. If you want to get her back, you need to do what we say. And we say you need to kill Salahnovich."

I shake his arm again. "I don't need to do anything. I have a hostage to trade."

Grigori shakes his head. "We don't negotiate. I have already sacrificed my life to this cause. It is forfeit. They will not try to get me back."

"What about the cargo?" I jerk my head toward the rear of the shuttle. "Your people won't survive without that."

His face droops the tiniest bit, then his expression hardens. "It is true we might lose a few people. But that is a sacrifice we're willing to make. And once you take out Salahnovich, my people can leave that hell hole and come back to civilization as heroes."

"You have way more faith in my ability to target a head of state than I do." I push him toward his corner of the hold. "Strap his hands to a crate, Arun."

Once Grigori is secure, we close the cargo hatch door and regroup in the shuttle. I turn to Leo. "We're going to leave you here to run interference. If anyone comes looking for Dima, he left an hour ago. If they want you to move the shuttle, tell them you've paid for a full day of parking." I raise a brow at Arun.

He nods. "I've got enough Gagarian credits to cover that."

"How did Dima get here? Can we steal his vehicle?" I study the dash, trying to identify the switch that will activate the external cams, but the dark buttons are unreadable.

"He came in an *autotaksi*. His left, but I have the app—but we'll be traceable."

I shrug. "No big deal. We aren't going to do anything that might get us in trouble. Certainly no assassinations."

Arun nods and flicks his app to order a vehicle.

I turn to Leo. "We might need you to come pick us up, so keep your audio on."

He taps the side of his head. "My implant has been a bit glitchy since we arrived here."

"Do you have a standard Commonwealth model?" I point at his holo-ring. "Run a diagnostic."

"I'm not sure it's standard." Leo flushes. "I had an experimental Leweian version when I left there. Had to have it removed and replaced without alerting anyone—"

"You have a black-market version." I close my eyes for a second. "When we get home, you're getting that replaced. It's too risky having unvetted hardware." I grab Grigori's chet from the dash and snap my fingers at Arun. "Grab Dima's will you? We can set these up with direct call."

Arun jogs to the galley and grabs the device we pulled from Dima's arm. He hands it to me. "How are we going to get out of this? Dima is my primary contact here. I'm supposed to be negotiating a deal with him on behalf of a huge consortium."

"I'm more worried about rescuing our friend than your business concerns." I glance up from the device with an apologetic face. "Sorry."

"No, you're right." He paces up and down the aisle as I work to connect the two chets.

Finally, I toss one at him. "You're the tech genius—can you do this?"

He catches the wrist strap against his chest, then sits down to get a closer look. "Shouldn't be too much trouble." After a few minutes, he lets out a "Ha!" and holds it out.

"You wear it." I shove the other one at Leo. "And you get this one. Stay out of sight as much as possible."

"No one should bother you." Arun tightens the communication device around his wrist and stands. He taps something on the tiny screen and grins. "Dima just paid your parking."

Leo smirks and flips Arun a jaunty salute. "Thank you, Dima!"

We exit the ship and head for the self-driving *autotaksi* that just pulled in beside the building in answer to Arun's order. The harsh wind makes me shiver, so I crank up the heat on my digital undies.

"Are you sure we can trust him?" Arun jerks his head back at the shuttle. "An hour ago, he was trying to force us to assassinate the secretary general."

"He wasn't trying to force us." I flick my holo-ring and bring up a vid. "He was trying to make it sound like he was forcing us. He knew Grigori's friends had Elodie and that they might be listening to us. Do you see this?" I stretch the vid bigger so he can see it, then start it playing. It shows the three of us inside the shuttle before we escaped the ice base. I zoom in, so he can see Leo's fingers. "See the tapping?"

Arun frowns at the vid. "Is that code?"

I nod. "I taught him and Elodie a few duress signals. That's the signal for 'observers.' Essentially, it means he's playing a role. He wants Grigori's folks to think he's on their side."

"Won't they be suspicious when he doesn't free Grigori as soon as we leave?" Arun swipes the *chet* against a panel in the *autotaksi's* fender, and the door pops open.

I hold a finger to my lips as we get into the car, then call Arun through my implant. "They might be. But their organization doesn't seem very… organized. He can fake communication problems. I think we can free Elodie and get back there before they can take any action against him. And remember what Grigori said—at this point, he's basically on a suicide mission."

We stare out the windows, watching the scenery pass by. Naunet was right about one thing—there's nothing interesting to see in this part of the Petrograd outskirts. Elodie's signal takes us to the center of town. The *autotaksi* deposits us in front of the People's Palace—the seat of government on Gagarin.

"She's here?" Arun stares up at the vast, blocky building. It sits on the far side of a huge, empty plaza. A few people walk around the edges of the open space, but no one strikes out across the center. There are no signs or barriers, but everyone skirts the edge. A long queue trails down one side.

I flick my holo-ring again, trying to keep my files small. Using our rings marks us as outsiders—only the ultra-wealthy on Gagarin have this tech. Using our bodies to shield my hands from view, I check Elodie's location, then nod. "Yes. This is also Salahnovich's current location. My guess is they expected us to find her, so they brought us as close to the target as they could. She's probably in one of the galleries."

According to the research I did before we came to Gagarin, the People's Palace contains multiple areas referred to as "galleries." Some of them display art. Others are seating areas that allow citizens to observe their government in action.

"Can we get in?" Arun looks around the square, then points. "That looks like a ticket sales kiosk."

I pull his hand down. "Don't draw attention. Tickets are free but usually reserved months in advance."

"Don't draw attention?" Arun gestures at me. "I think our clothing sets us apart."

I look down at my black, form-fitting clothes, then at the bulky coats worn by most of the women in the lines. Arun's garb blends in better, except his is obviously more luxurious. And our heated undergarments mean we don't have to wear multiple thick layers. I wish I'd brought a hat, though.

"How did your contact expect you to get in and—" He points a finger gun at me.

I grab his hand. His fingers are surprisingly warm against my cold ones. "How are your hands not freezing?"

He smiles. "ThermaSkin. I happen to know the CEO of Endure, and he gave me one to test when he heard I was coming to Gagarin."

Endure Clothing makes extreme weather gear, and they're currently beta testing tech that creates an invisible thermal layer around the wearer. It's like a heated blanket of air, which means the wearer doesn't need gloves or a hat. Or any clothing at all, in fact, but walking around nude would draw a lot of attention.

I'd love to get in on that beta. "And you didn't share?"

"Sorry, he only gave me one. Besides, you're so self-sufficient, it never occurred to me you'd need it." He wraps his big hand around my fingers, and the heat from the ThermaSkin skims over my hand and up my arm. "How are we going to get in?"

"Believe it or not, the message said tickets will be waiting for us at the kiosk."

"That sounds one hundred percent like a setup. The GIDK will be waiting for us to pick them up."

I lift a hand and rock it back and forth. "That part doesn't make me too nervous. For one thing, Grigori wants us to succeed, not get arrested before we do anything. And an anonymous ticket waiting at the kiosk is an easy way to get us in. They probably have them under different names almost every day—just in case they find a stooge to do their dirty work. Remember, originally, he was going to send me to the secretary general's residence as an employee. Clearly, they've set up multiple options." I yank on his hand, heading away from the Palace. "That doesn't mean we're not going to walk right into a potential trap."

"You have an alternate plan?"

I lead him to a little coffee shop across the street and order two cups. In a hilarious coincidence, this is Eliana's Bakery but not the location I needed before. We sit at a table near the door where we can watch the square through the window. I tap Arun's wrist. "I need you to make a call."

He pushes up his sleeve and presses a finger to the tiny screen. "You got a contact number?"

I nod and read it off to him. "It's Naunet. Or Risa--not sure which. We'll tell her we want to see the People's Palace today, but we don't have tickets."

He frowns at me, then shrugs and follows my instructions. A woman answers, her voice tinny through the cheap speaker. "Da?"

I lean across the table, putting my mouth close to his wrist. The warmth from the ThermaSkin tickles my lips. "Risa? This is Va—Lindsay Fioravanti. Can you get us into the People's Palace?"

TWENTY-EIGHT

I STARE out the bakery window as I wait for Risa's answer. Although her partner Naunet had spent time in the Commonwealth, my gut tells me Risa is more sympathetic to visitors. Or at least a fraction less likely to immediately report us to the government. Not that we've done anything worth reporting. Yet.

There's silence for a long moment, then Risa replies. "This day?"

"Yes. We're at the bakery across the square." I glance up at Arun and realize I'm awkwardly hunched over his arm.

"Soon. Wait." The call goes dead.

I sit up and lean back in my chair, lifting my coffee in toast.

Arun taps his plastek cup against mine. "Who was that?"

"Risa. She's one of the guides who showed me and Elodie around before."

His jaw drops. "You can't trust her! I can *guarantee* you she works for the government. They always assign foreign visitors 'guides' who can report back to them."

"Of course. That's what makes her perfect. No one would expect a Commonwealth agent to use official channels to get into their target location. Plus, it's not like I'm really going to—" I do my own finger gun.

His eyes pop, then he nods. "Good point. How'd you know she'd be available?"

I smirk. "Last time I gave her a huge tip. Cash."

"You know cash here is tracked, right? Digital codes embedded in the paper and metal."

I shake my head in dismay. "Who do you think you're dealing with? I brought older bills. They don't have the tracking. I'm sure Risa knows that too." I push against the table, shoving myself to my feet. "There she is."

Arun looks out the window, then stands. The tall blonde woman nods at us, then turns to look across the street at the Palace.

We put our cups in the recycler and exit the bakery, meeting Risa on the street. I shake hands with her, casually pressing another huge wad of untraceable cash into her palm, then introduce Arun only by his first name.

She gives him a quick once-over, her gaze flicking over the green bruise starting to bloom around his eye and to the sealed gashes in his lip. "I have heard of you. You bring new technology to Gagarin."

Arun flashes his million-credit top-lev smile, the sealant pulling it a little off center.

Risa puts a protective hand over her chet. "I don't like new technology."

Arun's smile dims.

"But trade is good for the country. Come." She turns away and hurries around the edge of the square toward the queue.

I catch up to Risa. "Why doesn't anyone cross the center of the square?"

She turns horrified eyes on me. "That is the grave of Petrov. No one would dare to walk on his grave."

"The whole plaza?" I sweep an arm at the vast space. "And who's Petrov?"

She stops dead, turning to stare at me. "Who is Petrov? He saved the entire people of Gagarin! The city is named for him! How is—you do not know of Petrov in the Commonwealth?"

I raise both hands, palms out. "Nope. You didn't mention him at the Hall of Heroes."

"Petrov is bigger than the Hall of Heroes." She turns away, muttering under her breath as she leads us around the end of the queue and past the people waiting. The line doesn't appear to have moved. I noted the locations of a few specific individuals when we arrived, and after thirty minutes in the bakery, they're still in the same frigid spots.

The queue goes up the wide steps, staying tight against the right end. Other people stream in and out of the half dozen heavy metal doors, but they all wear badges. Based on their utilitarian attire, they're likely government flunkies.

When we reach the front of the line, I see why it hasn't moved. A window beside the front doors has a speaker and a pass-through—probably for tickets—but the shades are closed. Written in both Gagarin and bad Standard, it says something about a lunch break.

Risa bypasses the dark window and knocks on the nearest door. Unlike the metal ones the employees use, this one is dark glass. It opens a few centimeters, and Risa holds a whispered conversation with someone inside. She taps her chet, then reaches into her pocket. I can't see what she's got in her fist as she pushes her hand through the narrow gap, but my bet is on cash. My cash—but probably not all of it.

The doors open wider.

"This way." Risa stomps through the opening.

I glance back at the line, expecting a protest, but no one seems particularly surprised or interested. With a shrug, I follow Risa into the building. Arun closes in behind, and the door shuts with a soft whomp.

We've entered a small vestibule. A fishy smell assaults us, making my eyes water. I stare around the room, looking for a source for the stench. Plain white walls bear multiple signs in blocky Gagarian letters. A quick scan reveals they're warning visitors not to touch anything or speak to anyone inside. Silence is required. At the far end of the small space, another double door—this time metal like the others—waits.

The man who let us in settles into his chair beside the outer door, a thick sandwich gripped in both hands. Little chunks of white drop onto his gray sweater, coming to rest on his sizable paunch. He says something to Risa, jerking his head at the inner door, then picks up the loose cubes and pops them into his mouth.

Risa responds, then turns to wave us forward. "Come."

The inner doors lead to a vast entrance hall. A long red rope, held by brassy stanchions, keeps us to one side of the room. To our left, three pairs of double doors open and close as badge-wearing employees enter. As one swings wide, I catch a glimpse of security guards running hand-held scanners over individuals, then waving them on. The visitors pause beside a long, boxy machine to grab their bags from a conveyor belt.

I initiate a private call to Arun. "We didn't go through security."

He jerks his head back at the doors through which we entered. "I think our fishy friend back there was supposed to check us."

Risa stops and spreads her arms wide to encompass the vast echoing chamber. "This is grand entry. Tiles of the floor were being crafted—" Shoes clatter against the slick tile floors. Smooth stone walls amplify the sound, creating a deafening cacophony. Risa's waving arms draw the attention of a worker passing behind her. The woman makes eye contact with me, then her gaze darts away as if hoping I hadn't noticed her.

I tune out Risa's stilted speech to speak with Arun. "We need to get away from her."

"Won't she raise an alarm if we disappear?" He looks around the big room. "Besides, where are we going to go?"

I turn to watch the steady stream of employees trudging down the hall. At the far end, our roped-off section ends, directing visitors through an inelegant arch. The ropes prevent visitors from taking the wide steps to the second floor or one of the corridors branching off to either side. I start moving toward the end of the viewing area. "Where does this go?"

Risa hurries to catch up, pointing through the opening. "The visitors' gallery is up there."

As we reach the end of the hall, I can see through the arch to stairs leading upward. Heavy doors are propped open to allow visitors easy access. Risa stops. "We can go up, but you must be quiet."

"I want to go that way." I point over the red rope to the wide steps the employees tromp up and down. "That stairway would make a great backdrop for a vid."

Risa's mouth goes slack. She snaps her jaw shut and shakes her head. "No. You are not the vid woman. There is no drones in this building."

I giggle, putting on my Lindsay persona. "You're right, I'm not the vid woman. And don't worry, I don't have any drones running. But Elodie asked me to get some good images. Arun can use his chet to take them, okay?" Without waiting for a reply, I duck under the rope and run to the wide steps. A man wearing a long, heavy overcoat glares at me but says nothing as he changes directions to avoid me.

I get halfway up the wide steps and turn, arms out, a big smile on my face. "Get a still, Arun!"

"Hush!" Risa whisper-shouts as she and Arun hurry toward me. "Come down from there! Visitors must not—"

I bend and drop my hands to my knees, turning a shoulder toward them in a coy pose I've seen all over social media. Pushing my lips out in an air kiss, I shimmy a little. "Did you get the pic?"

Arun stops at the bottom of the steps, staring up at me, hands lifted in confusion. "Get a pic with what?"

"Your chet. It can take stills, can't it?" I lift one hand over my head and turn a little to the side. "How's this?"

"You must come down from there!" Risa thunders up the steps.

I wait until she's almost within grabbing distance, then I sprint up to the second floor. "What's up here?"

Swearing under her breath, Risa hurries after me, moving surprisingly quickly for a woman of her stature.

Arun trails behind. "What do you want me to do?" His calm question comes through my audio implant.

I look around the second floor. The wide steps end at a low-ceilinged lobby. The few employees who took the steps turn off into the side stairways leading higher, but no one takes the narrow corridor that leads deeper into the building.

My tracking app tells me Elodie is down that hallway. I stride along as if I belong here, not pausing to read any of the many multi-language signs posted between the widely spaced doors. I reach the fourth one on the right and stop. My translation software does its thing, cataloging the Gagarian letters and replacing them with Standard. "This is the justice court."

Risa's hand locks onto my wrist. "You cannot go in there. Visitors must use the viewing gallery." She points back the way we came.

"But Elodie is in there." My software has pinpointed her location, but I still can't connect an audio call.

Arun stops behind Risa, his hand sliding into his pocket where he keeps his stunner. I give a tiny headshake to stop him from pulling it out. He glances behind, but there's no one in sight. He raises a brow, clearly suggesting, "We can take her."

I reply through our still-active call. "I don't want to take her out." I pull another wad of cash from my pocket and hand it to Risa. "Please, can you get us in there? Someone is holding Elodie hostage."

"Where'd you get so many credits?" Arun asks aloud. "You were holding out. You could have paid for the *autotaksi*."

"They don't take cash." Risa releases my arm to grab the bills and shove them into the pocket of her voluminous coat. "How do you find Elodie?"

I smirk and reach for the doorknob. "I can't tell you that. But I know she's in there."

Risa steps between me and the door, pulling a stunner from her cash pocket. "Do your job and we give her back."

TWENTY-NINE

I GAPE at the tall blonde woman blocking the door to the justice court. "What?"

Risa can't possibly know why Grigori's people abducted Elodie.

"You are here to free us from Salahnovich. Do that, and we give your friend back." Risa crosses her arms.

I stand corrected.

"You're working with Grigori?" Arun asks, his incredulous question echoing down the hall.

We both shush him.

I glare at Risa. "I can't do that. How do you expect me to get a weapon anywhere near him?"

Risa just stares at me. Then her gaze drops to my ankle, where she apparently knows I keep my spare stunner. "I got your weapon in."

I rub my forehead. Has Grigori been pulling the strings all along? He must have caused Risa to be assigned to our tour on that first day. Then he grabbed Leo to force us to find him. Our little detour to Yussupova Northern Base might have thrown them off, but now we're back on track. They have a hostage, and they have their assassin in place. Me.

Risa jerks the stunner at me. "Do your job, or I shoot your friend. It is set to highest power."

Behind me, Arun starts to back away, but Risa waves the weapon again. "No. She must do this for all of us."

"Why do you think killing Salahnovich is going to solve all of your problems?" I toggle my audio and whisper to Arun, "Get behind me."

"I am behind you, but I'm a lot bigger than you. Even here, I make a great target."

Risa speaks over Arun's silent response. "He is leader of the current regime. Killing him makes chaos. We get new leader. Leader we choose."

"You think they aren't prepared for that? According to my information, there are a dozen succession plans for Salahnovich." I take a slow step back, my foot hitting Arun's.

"Yes, dozen people who think, 'I am leader.' They will fight. We will win." Risa opens the door behind her, then reaches out to grab my arm. "You do job. Now."

I can't really argue with her theory because I thought the same thing. Salahnovich's death will result in chaos. If Grigori's people have prepped for this, they could take over. But that doesn't mean I want to pull the trigger. I lean back, refusing to follow her into the room. "You do it."

She lets go of my arm, and I stumble back into Arun.

"I like this idea." Risa spins and stalks into the room.

I spin and slap a hand against Arun's arm. "Run! Get back to the shuttle! I'll get Elodie."

"I'm not going anywhere." He shakes off my hand and uses his body to push me toward the door Risa just disappeared through. "Elodie is on Gagarin because I brought her, and I'm going to make sure she gets home."

"Ugh, fine. But do as I say." I have little hope he'll actually follow my directions—the chivalry trained into him in his youth tends to overcome his belief that I know what the zark I'm doing. But I have to try. I push the door open again.

It leads to a dark hallway. At the far end, another door stands ajar, light streaming around the edges. A harsh voice speaks in long, uninterrupted phrases—probably a speech of some kind. I race toward the door, then drop to a crouch before pushing it far enough to see inside.

Rows of seats stretch to either side, in tiers down to an ornate railing in a U-shaped gallery around this end of the room. Steps form an aisle from our door to the front row of seats. A huge stained-glass dome arches overhead. In bright sunlight, it's probably spectacular, but today the colors are muted. Below, a man stands behind a podium, ranting and gesturing, spit flying from his lips. Spotlights glare down, leaving the rest of the room in dim shadow. A low rumble underscores the words as many voices punctuate the speech with agreement. Fifteen or twenty visitors sit on the far side, but none of them look up as we enter.

Risa stalks down the steps, her hand in her pocket.

In the bottom row, near the wall, Elodie sits by the railing. She wears brightly patterned pants, in colors that would rival the glass dome on a sunny day, and a fluorescent green top. The cam pinned in her hair gives me a partially obstructed view of the room below. I try to connect with her audio again but am denied. She could have a dozen tinfoil hats hidden in that unruly cloud of rainbow hued hair.

Two men sit with her, one blocking her access to the aisle, the other behind. They all turn to look when the door clicks shut. Three pairs of eyes lock onto me. Risa doesn't even twitch.

Elodie waves. "Hi, Vanti!"

"Shush!" Both men spin around to hush her. With their backs to me, I fire two stunner blasts, and they slump in their seats.

Across the room, some of the visitors watch us. When I make eye-contact, they look away, returning their attention to the angry man on the stage. Two guards leave their posts beside the door and race along the top tier toward the empty end of the gallery. Risa continues down the steps, seeming oblivious to anything but her target.

Down on the floor, the speaker drones on. I pause halfway down the steps. A faint shimmer beyond the balcony indicates a force field. A quick scan through my oc-lens confirms it provides one-way audio dampening as well as a physical barrier. Based on the arching shape, it's probably projected from the domed ceiling. If I were trying to accomplish Grigori's mission, I'd find the projectors and take them out, but that's Risa's problem, not mine.

"We've got incoming." I move across a row to intercept them. My stunner has a long range, but the force shield angles upward, blocking the shot.

Arun scrabbles at his buckle, trying to remove the extra grav-belt we brought for Elodie. "The latch is stuck."

I grit my teeth. I shouldn't have let him carry the spare, but he wanted to help. "Do you need help?"

Elodie giggles as she climbs over the prone guard blocking her aisle. "Vanti can help you unbuckle your belt, Arun."

My ears get hot, but I ignore the sensation. The first of the guards has crossed the end of the U-shaped gallery and started down the steps toward us. I wait until the second one has cleared the force field, then fire at him first.

The closer guard returns fire. I've already moved, and his shot goes wide. He throws himself into a row of seats. He's well trained—he didn't look to see if his partner went down.

He did, of course.

A few of the citizens watching the speech glance at the commotion, but most of them remain resolutely focused on the speaker. I catch a couple angling their chets to take vid of us, while keeping their heads turned to the front of the room. As a group, they seem to contract, every person moving a few seats farther from the action. Their dedication to not getting involved is impressive.

Risa grips the edge of the wide stone balcony, leaning over to look. She must decide she doesn't have the mass to break through the force shield, because she looks up, her gaze going to the corners of the arched roof.

"Arun, as soon as I take out the last guard, get Elodie to the other side. If Risa's really going to do this, we need to try to blend in. And for zark's sake, get her to turn off the rainbow hair!"

"Roger." Arun's response is quick and professional—almost as good as working with Griz. "We need backup."

"We don't have backup."

"Too bad we don't have one of those fake posse apps like your friend had at TechnoTropolis."

"I can't believe—" With a mental forehead slap, I flick my holo-ring and activate *4ssMultiplier*. I set "environment" to "hostile—under fire," and the "minion level" to 3. Realistic holograms appear—two nearby and a third halfway between me and the cowering guard on the upper level. They wear black clothing and carry blasters and stunners. Two of them crouch behind chairs, and the third lies flat in an aisle.

"I'm not sure they're going to help much. They can't shoot." I watch the seats where the guard hid, catching a glimpse of him just before he pops up to fire. He's fast, but I'm faster. "Second guard is down. We need to move before their backup arrives. And we need an exit plan."

"Working on it."

What does that mean? I don't have time to ask as we race toward the far end of the room. My faux friends follow behind, backing between the rows, weapons at the ready. I yank off my jacket as I wait at the bottom of the corner stairway. "Here." I shove the jacket into Elodie's hands as they shuffle past me. Her hair is already a mousy brown, but the brilliant clothing will make her a target. "Tone down the rainbow clothes."

"Vanti," a voice whispers in my ear.

"Elodie?" I run up the steps to relieve the closer guard of his weapon. He's an older guy—probably part of a reserve unit—and only has a stunner. I debate detouring to the one on the top row. Too far. I shuffle sideways along the row of seats. Below me, Arun and Elodie hurry along the wider space between the front row and the railing. The 4ssMultipliers bring up the rear.

"No, it's Helva."

I choke back my urge to cheer. "Where are you?"

Risa takes aim at one of the force shield transmitters. She fires, and sparks shower down, drawing the attention of people in the gallery. They surge to their feet, scrambling over the seats and up the steps to the door.

"Zark."

The speaker continues haranguing his audience, oblivious to the danger. That force shield might have a visual component too—at least from his side.

"I'm at Bondarenko's," Helva says. "There's another shuttle here—it's registered to someone called Nortov."

"That's Grigori's ship. Leo and the cat are there—get them aboard. Then we'll need an emergency extraction from the People's Palace."

Helva whistles. "That is not going to make me very popular with the locals. Are you sure of that?"

Risa fires another shot at the force shield transmitter. Sirens blare. Behind us, the door opens and guards tumble through. They check at the sight of my squad—which chooses that moment to glitch. One of the entering soldiers fires, his blast ripping through my fake rear guard and singing the stone balustrade. Ahead, someone screams, and the exodus from the gallery turns into a stampede. No guards are getting in that way—at least not for a few minutes.

"Come on!" Arun yells back at me as he and Elodie start up the steps.

"Yes, I'm sure," I tell Helva. "We've got a revolutionary about to attempt an assassination, and we need to get out!"

"Roger. Leo is en route to me. I've got eyes on him."

"You don't have eyes, Helva."

Risa spins and fires at the security personnel coming down the steps behind her. Plaster flies from the door frame. The guards dive aside without returning fire. Spinning, Risa puts a hand on the stone railing and vaults over, landing on the force shield with a thud. It holds.

As a firefight between Risa and the guards erupts behind me, I leap onto the arm rest of the closest chair and run down the row, keeping low. A few blaster shots come close, but none of them hit me.

"Vanti, incoming!" Arun screams.

THIRTY

Reaching the end of the row, I dive to the steps. My shoulder slams into the wide tread, and I tuck my head and roll up the stairs. Ignoring the throbbing pain, I push to my feet, remaining crouched behind the closest chair.

I toggle my audio. "Arun, does Elodie have any drones?"

After a brief pause, Arun responds. "Negative. Just the cam on her hairpin."

Normally I'd have several, but I haven't had a chance to restock. I poke my head over the tops of the chairs for a quick look. Three guards have shoved through the outflow of people ahead of us. Several civilians lie nearby, stunned by the security guys trying to get into the room. Crouched near the bottom of the gallery, almost directly below the entry, Arun fires wildly. The stun beam splashes against the door. The guards dive behind the top row of seats. The few remaining civilians scream and lunge for the exit.

One of the guards grabs an old man and uses him as a shield. He yells something in Gagarian, his blaster waving at the man's head.

"Stun the old man," I tell Arun.

"What? I'm not going to shoot a helpless victim."

"You'll be doing him a favor. If that guard fires at that range, it will kill him. Your stunner will just take him down. Now." I take aim, waiting.

Arun drops to his belly and peeks around the legs of the last chair. He fires up the steps, hitting the old man squarely in the chest. As his human shield slumps in his arms, I hit the guard in the head. Both men crumple to the stone floor.

Behind us, Risa exchanges fire with the uniformed men at the top of the steps. Every third shot, she fires at the force shield emitters. Sparks fly, and one of the emitters goes out in a flash. Below, the lawmakers glance up in horror, finally noticing the commotion above their heads.

"We're trapped." A thread of panic underscores Arun's words.

"It looks bad, but we still have options." I take out the second soldier above us. "When I get that last guy, be ready to run. Does Elodie have her grav-belt on?"

"Yup." Elodie's voice comes through this time. "I got rid of the tinfoil hat too."

"Perfect. On my mark. Three, two—" The last civilian tumbles backward through the door, shoved by a team of black-clothed commandos. "Zark." I fire a few shots, just to keep them down. "Over the balcony! Grav-belts on emergency setting."

"Emergency setting on," Arun confirms.

"Over the balcony?" Elodie shrieks.

"There's a force shield." I scramble down the steps toward the railing.

"There's also a bunch of bad guys down there," Elodie wails, pointing.

I reach the stone balustrade and peer between the carved uprights. "Those are lawmakers. They aren't dangerous. Besides, the force shield will protect us." I fire a few cover shots and dive over the railing.

My bruised shoulder slams into the invisible shield with as much force as hitting the floor. I grit my teeth and roll to my feet. Using the stone railing for cover, I take out one of the new commandos. "Get over here. Now!"

My stunner pings with the low power alert. I get off a few more shots, taking down two soldiers, but a seemingly unending supply rushes into the room. Arun shoves Elodie over the wide rail, then dives after. He yelps as a beam hits his foot.

"Are you injured?" I fire back, but my weapon is dead.

"No, but these loafers will never be the same."

Below us, chaos reigns. A few remaining lawmakers cower behind their desks as their coworkers jam the doors, yelling and crying. Risa swears and fires at the force shield emitters again. The one she's been concentrating on finally explodes, and the "floor" beneath us lurches.

"Those things are connected." I duck and race across the invisible surface to crouch beside Arun. "The others are compensating, but if another one goes, we'll fall."

Arun pats his belt. "That's what these are for, right?"

I nod and hold out a hand. "You got a stunner charge?"

He slaps his weapon into my palm. "No. This one's still at fifty percent."

Behind us, Risa swears again. Sparks shower down from the emitter above our heads, and we duck even lower. I aim between the uprights and take down another commando. He's replaced by three more.

I check the charge on the stunner. Down to forty. "Helva, what's your ETA? We're going to need extraction sooner than later."

There's no answer from the shuttle.

"We need to get out of the building first." Arun ducks as a blaster beam singes the stone we cower behind.

"Then we need to go up." Elodie points at the stained-glass dome.

"We need a blaster to break through that." I knew I should have taken the time to disarm the other guard. But there was no guarantee he had anything more lethal than his partner. "Can you reach Helva?"

Elodie shakes her head. "Negative. She must still be aboard the *Ostelah*."

I frown. Why did Helva contact me instead of Arun? A blaster beam distracts me. I take aim through the balusters, and another soldiers collapses. Thirty-four percent.

The force shield shakes beneath us. "Go to full grav-belt. Set it at —" I look at my control screen and try to use the app to measure the distance to the floor. "I can't tell how high we are."

"Use current position." Arun flicks something on his own holo-ring.

I close my eyes for a second, berating my own stupidity. "Good call. Keep trying Helva." I send a quick message to the shuttle, telling her Arun is on our side. When we last spoke, she wasn't sure.

Which is really odd. A computer—even one as advanced as Helva—shouldn't be able to ignore their owner. I make a mental note to have Arun check Helva's programming when we get back.

More blaster fire forces us down. I fire again, taking down two more. My stunner is at eighteen percent.

A woman screams.

"They got Risa!" Elodie cries. "We need to help her!"

"We can't!" Arun grabs Elodie as she starts to rise and pulls her back down. "And set your grav-belt. That force shield could still give out at any second!"

Quiet falls, as if the soldiers have realized we're not shooting back. A voice blares at us in Gagarian, barking orders. I glance at Arun, my brows raised.

"They want us to come out with our hands up."

"Not gonna happen. I don't trust Gagarians not to shoot us." I raise my voice and holler, "We'll accept your surrender now!"

Elodie giggles, but it has a hysterical edge.

"Come out. Now." This time, the words are in heavily accented Standard. "We have you surrounded."

Time to reevaluate our position. Four soldiers edge slowly down the far side. I take careful aim and manage to hit one. The others duck aside as their companion falls to the steps. "I can do this all day!" I yell.

"No, you can't." Arun puts a hand on my wrist, drawing my attention to the flashing red indicator on the weapon. "We're done."

"They aren't going to let us go. As far as they're concerned, we were part of an attempt on their leader's life. If we put so much as a finger over that railing, they will shoot us dead." My heart pounds in my chest. I've been close to death before, but I've never brought innocent victims—my friends—with me before. I've always had an escape plan. But this time, I'm coming up empty.

"Then what are we going to do?" Elodie whispers.

"We're going up." I point at the glass ceiling. "Set your belt to emergency jump zeta. Launch two seconds behind me."

"We can't get through that glass. It's got to be reinforced. They must be prepared for an overhead attack." Arun's hand tightens on my arm.

"They're expecting an *external* attack. That doesn't mean they're prepared for anything trying to get out. The force of my jump will shatter the glass." I don't tell him what it will do to my head. "When you get out, go to Bondarenko's. Helva was there. And if she isn't, you can use Grigori's shuttle."

Arun looks up at the glass dome, then back at me. "Hitting that ceiling will kill you. You won't make it."

"My job isn't to 'make it.' It's to make sure Elodie gets out. And you."

"I can't let you do that."

I flick my holo-ring and bring up the controls for their grav-belts. Setting them to launch with zeta-bravo two seconds after me, then disconnect, I hit the lock. "You don't get to make that decision."

Then I twist my arm out of his grip, fling it over my head, and hit the emergency jump sequence.

THIRTY-ONE

I'M NOT afraid of heights, and I have lots of experience with grav-belts, but emergency jump sequence zeta makes my blood run cold. The launch redlines—faster than a human should go, putting tremendous G-forces on the body. Here on Gagarin, where gravity is slightly higher than normal, it's even worse. When you add in the fact that my head is about to take out a reinforced glass ceiling, you can see why this is not my favorite option.

The grav-belt slams me upward. I hunch my shoulders and hope my left arm will take the brunt of the force. I'm moving so fast I can't get my right arm up to help, so I squeeze my eyes shut and pray.

An ear-splitting wail bites into my brain like an unsharpened buzz-saw trying to cut platinum. Glass shatters, pelting me like hail, jabbing my arm and face, and then I'm through. Wind whistles in my ears, freezing the tips. A shadow falls over me, but I can't turn my head to see the cause.

"Did you see that?" an excited voice cries through my audio implant. "I broke the glass with just the sound of my voice!"

"Helva? Where are you?" Tears stream from my eyes. I force them wider, but everything is blurry.

"I'm right over your head," Helva says smugly. "At the projected apex of your jump. You should be able to step right in."

As I approach the top of the sequence, my speed decreases, and I'm able to move my arms again. I swipe the tears away before they can freeze on my face. A mix of tears and blood freezes on my fingers. "Elodie and Arun?"

"They're right behind you."

I look down, picking out the tops of their heads as they speed away from the destroyed roof of the People's Palace. The massive building spreads out below, covering several city blocks. Dozens of dark glass domes sprout from the flat roof. Helva managed to shatter not just the dome through which we exited, but three others nearby. As I watch, a fourth one crumbles, the protective gray external glass falling on the colorful art beneath. I hold my breath, but the brighter panels stay intact.

"We need to get out of Dodge. They are going to send us to Xinjianestan for damaging national treasures. How did you do it?" I reach the top of my upward arc, and the system keeps me at this altitude. I set my forward speed and direction and aim for Helva's open rear ramp.

I come in hot. Helva is hovering above the Palace, but I misjudged the distance. I blame my still blurry eyesight. I slap the emergency stop control and drop to the deck of the cargo hold, hitting hard. My knee buckles under me, and I collapse in a pile on the cold floor.

Arun and Elodie drop to the deck a bit more gracefully. Zeta-bravo launch isn't quite as forceful as straight up zeta, so they had a bit more time to adjust. Still, for amateurs, they did a good job sticking the landing. I start to rise, but my head swims and my leg refuses to cooperate.

"Vanti!" Arun stumbles across the deck to me.

"Get us out of here!" I push feebly, trying to send him to the front of the ship. Pain explodes through my body as if it had been waiting until we were safe and is now doubling down. I clamp my eyes shut and bite back a whimper.

"I'm on it." Elodie hurries past as the rear ramp hinges closed.

"Take your time," Helva says aloud. "Leo and the cat are here. Besides, I've got it covered."

I wipe a hand over my face, my fingers coming away bloody. Arun crouches beside me, his expression grave and his face pale. "Are you—where are you hurt?" He looks at my leg and gasps. "That is not supposed to bend that way!"

His face seems to float before my eyes, going all washy and translucent. Darkness wraps around me, leaving only his face visible. Then it's gone too.

WHEN I COME TO, I'm in a med pod. The lid clicks, and an androgynous voice says, "Health restored. Please exercise caution over the next two days. No heavy lifting, no alcohol or recreational drugs, no sexual activity."

"Thanks." If my health is restored, why place restrictions on me? The lid retracts, and I sit up, rolling my shoulders and twisting my back. Everything feels normal. I swing my legs out of the pod and spot Arun sitting on a chair in the corner of the *Ostelah*'s small medical suite. "Good morning."

"It's afternoon." A little smile plays around the corners of his lips. "I had Elodie get some clothes from your cabin." He nods at a pile of black fabric on the counter next to him.

I look down at the paper-thin medical gown covering me. The cheerful daisies make me cringe. I don't wear flowers. "How long was I out?"

"Twenty-seven hours."

My eyes go wide. "For a few glass cuts? Where are we?"

"You had way more than a few glass cuts. A couple of the larger shards pierced your chest and abdomen, causing major damage. Plus, your right knee must have hit something on the way out—it required significant reconstructive surgery. Luckily, I have the best med pod credits can buy, so it's probably better than the original."

I push myself over the lip of the pod, my bare feet hitting the cold deck. Some experimental movements confirm the knee's stability. "It feels great."

Arun looks away, his cheeks flushed. "You might want to get dressed before you—" He waves a hand vaguely at me. "That gown is a bit revealing."

I look down. My lunge has caused the gown to ride up high on my thighs, but all of the important bits are still covered. With a snort, I straighten and allow the fabric to fall almost to my knees. "Are you bashful?"

Arun glances at me and quickly away. "Not really, but I prefer a less clinical environment if I'm going to see a beautiful woman's body."

My ears go hot. He thinks I'm beautiful.

Avoiding his gaze, I gather up the clothing he indicated earlier and realize he didn't answer my question. "Where are we?"

"We're almost to the jump belt. Helva connected to the *Ostelah* and flew it away from the station without a crew! Without being directed. I don't know how she managed it, but I'm going to find out." He looks more admiring than concerned, but the idea that an AI controlled shuttle could take command of an unmanned vessel is disturbing. What else can Helva do?

I've been operating under the assumption Helva is just a really sophisticated computer system, but if that's the case, would she have tried that trick? A shuttle's primary job is to move people and equipment from the surface of a planet to a ship in orbit or docked at a station. Calculating outside those parameters should be beyond her capabilities. How much autonomy does she have?

"She did that on her own?" There I go—anthropomorphizing her again.

"She suggested it but waited for me to approve the plan."

"That doesn't worry you?" I glance at the overhead. Thanks to patient privacy rights, the medical suite on any Commonwealth vehicle or station is supposed to be completely private, but I suspect Helva can listen in if she wants.

"It concerns me a bit, but there's not a lot I can do about it right now."

"Are we out of the system? Anyone chasing us?"

Arun lifts a hand and rocks it back and forth. "We're on our way to the jump belt. A couple of military ships came after us, but they can't keep up with the *Ostelah*. I considered an emergency jump—this ship has the power and equipment to manage it, but I figured we've already created enough of an international incident. You know, what with destroying their seat of government."

I wave that off. "We broke a few windows."

With a smirk, he turns to the door. "Jump in about two hours."

"And everyone is aboard?"

"Leo and the cat were in Helva when she picked us up. Wow, that sounds really wrong." His smile fades. "Raynaud is locked in his cabin." He pounds his fist softly against the door, once.

I touch his arm. "Sorry about him. I can't believe our background checks didn't find his Gagarian connections."

He nods and opens the door. "I should have done a better job checking. He's been with the company for years, though, and I wasn't too worried about security back then. I was more concerned with skills and work ethic. Was he a sleeper agent, or did they turn him? I'll leave you to get dressed." He pulls away and shuts the door quietly, leaving me alone.

I make use of the lav cubicle here in the medical suite, then look in the mirror. My body is clean, and no scars mar my pale skin. The lacerations on my face and arms have healed, leaving no trace, as expected with a high-end med pod. I run a comb through my hair. The coppery strands look healthy, but some odd chunks have gone missing. I smooth the shaggy ends, then pull it back into my customary tail at the nape of my neck. I'll have to find a salon at our next stop. I may wear mostly black, but I'm a bit vain about my hair.

After getting dressed, I make my way to the lounge, but it's empty. A quick tour of the ship reveals why—everyone is on the bridge. Which is a ridiculously grand name for a space not much bigger than the shuttle.

I pause in the open doorway. Leo and Elodie sit in the pilot and copilot seats, conferring over something. Apawllo has taken his now customary position across the top of Elodie's seat back. Arun perches in the jump seat behind Elodie. He looks up and smiles, sweeping a hand toward the other jump seat. "It's not fancy, but you should probably sit down for jump."

Elodie spins at the sound of his voice and lurches out of her seat. "Vanti! You're okay!" She wraps me in a warm hug, squeezing gently as if she's afraid I might break.

"I'm glad you're okay too." My arms tighten—just for a second. I don't want her to think I've gone soft. "Did you get your turn in the med pod before they kidnapped you again?"

She looks away.

I swing around to point a finger at Arun. "You should have put her in the med pod first!"

He lifts both hands. "She had a turn—before Raynaud kidnapped her."

I swing back to Elodie. "You didn't get cut in the falling glass?"

She touches her smooth cheek. "I did, but a med-wand took care of it. Did Helva tell you what she did?"

Before I can response, Helva jumps in. "I broke the glass dome with just the sound of my voice." An image of a beautiful woman wearing a flowing gown and flowers in her hair appears. She takes a deep breath, sings a pure, clear note, and the wine glass in her hand shatters.

"Oh, that. Yeah, I heard." I perch on the seat Arun pulled down. "Just your voice, huh?"

The image nods regally.

I hide a grin. "You don't have a sonic blaster?"

The holo-woman lifts her chin and tosses her hair back. "I broke that glass by singing."

"Sure." I raise a brow at Arun who smiles back.

"I saw that!" The singer disappears.

"Since you don't have vocal chords—"

"Oh, shut up," Helva snaps. "Forward jump shield engaged."

"Hey, just because you *can* pilot this ship remotely doesn't mean you should," Elodie tells the AI.

"I can do it better than you can. And it's not really remote since I'm docked to the ship." Helva tosses a diagram of the ship onto the forward screen, the location of the shuttle ringed in a rainbow glow.

"It's remote if you aren't in the cockpit." Elodie crosses her arms.

Leo clears his throat. "Jump in five minutes. You wanna strap in, Vanti?"

I pull the lap belt across my legs. Incidents rarely occur during jump anymore, but I'm not above taking precautions when available. The last time I thought jumping was "safe," my friends were transported to another dimension. After I snap the buckle, I cross my fingers.

"Zark!" Leo and Elodie yell together. The ship jinks so hard and so fast it takes the artificial gravity a few seconds to catch up. The ship's schematic slides aside, revealing an enormous ship barreling straight toward us. It seems to veer off to the side as we dive away.

As the other ship slides out of view, Elodie clutches her chest. "Where the heck did that come from?"

"They jumped in," Helva says. "Someone probably messaged the Gagarian outpost near Tereshkova. It's closer to the jump belt than their bases here. Don't worry, I'm taking evasive action."

"But this is the outward-bound belt!" Elodie swipes through screens, doing who knows what. "They can't jump *in* here!"

"In-bound and out-bound are just designations. You can go either direction as long as you're within the radius of the—" A tinge of anxiety marks Helva's voice, as if she's valiantly holding it together in the face of high stakes. Which she is. Except she's a machine. Her mimicry of human emotion is impressive.

I mean *it*. *Its* mimicry is impressive.

Elodie smacks the dash. "I know that! But they could have hit us head-on! That thing is huge. We woulda been toast."

"That was probably the plan." Arun unbuckles his belt. "Leo, switch with me. I have more stick time than you."

As the two men swap places, Elodie's screens go dark. "Hey!"

"I got this," Helva says. "I can do evasive maneuvers faster than any human."

"How *did* you get control of the ship?" Arun snaps the metal latch on his restraints. "You're the *shuttle's* OS, not the ship's."

"Same way I brought the *Ostelah Veesta* out to meet us. The ship's OS is as dumb as a box of asteroids. I told it to get out of the way and it did." Satisfaction oozes through Helva's voice. "The enemy ship is reducing acceleration. It looks like they're going to reverse course rather than coming around. It's what I'd do if I were that big."

A real-time tactical display lights up on the forward screens. The *Ostelah* shows as a bright pinpoint of green light diving toward the exit jump belt around Gagarin's primary. The military cruiser, designated by a poop emoji, pulls away behind us, slowing visibly.

"Where did you get this display software, Helva?" Arun asks.

"The cruiser's weapon systems are coming online." Helva's usually chipper voice has taken on a brusque tone. "That's a Leonov frigate—it has pulse cannons aft. If they get them online before we jump, we're space dust. I recommend you all relocate to the shuttle. My hull is small enough that they might find it difficult to target us at this range."

"Are you saying we should abandon ship?" Elodie asks.

"Yes."

"That ship will be able to target your hull, Helva." Arun pulls up a screen full of dense data and line drawings. "I have the schematics for the Leonov. They've got advanced micro-targeting with osmium gamma-wave impulse technology."

Helva hums, as if thinking. "I guess you'd have a better chance of survival if you stay aboard the *Ostelah*. Let me noodle on this for a second."

"They're pointing weapons at us, Helva. Noodle quickly!"

I tap Arun's shoulder. "Where did you get the schematics for a Leonov? Those are highly classified." And recently added to the CCIA's data banks—via a certain data drop at Super Annoying Funland. "Did you copy those when we—" I bite my tongue—I can't discuss classified information with him.

Arun turns innocent puppy eyes on me. "Who, me? When would I have done that?"

An analog gauge appears above the tactical display, indicating our speed. The pointer edges toward the blue "jump window" section on the right. Beside it, a digital countdown glows in huge red numbers with a label that reads "in range of weapons." A red wedge blinks on the tactical display with the apex centered on the poop emoji and the arc a few centimeters from the *Ostelah's* green star. Another digital countdown appears beside the jump window gauge, this one a few seconds behind the first. If these are correct, we'll reach jump speed *after* we come into range of the Leonov's weapon system.

"Got it!" Helva says. "I'm going to draw them off. They'll think you're trying to escape. I've got the *Ostelah* programmed to jump the instant it reaches critical transport speed." The diagram of the ship slides to the center of the screen, drawing our attention as the shuttle launches, still encircled in the rainbow glow.

"But they'll shoot you down!" Arun lunges against his restraints, but there's nothing he can do.

On the tactical display, the red wedge brushes against the green dot of the ship just as a bright pink comet shoots away on a perpendicular course.

"They can't catch me!" Helva crows as the pink dot becomes a tiny unicorn-shaped icon and begins a series of crazy swoops and spirals. "Without you softshells aboard, I don't have to waste power protecting you from high-G maneuvers."

"Don't go too wild," I caution. "They won't believe we're aboard if you're doing something humans can't withstand."

"Don't try to teach grandma to suck eggs, Vanti. I know exactly what humans can take, and I'm staying barely within the parameters."

The red wedge jinks to the side, centering on the shuttle now as the cruiser changes vectors. The trailing corner of the arc ticks over our green dot, and the "in range" countdown flips to zero. An alert klaxon howls and is silenced. The arc moves beyond us.

"But how will you get back to us?" Arun asks.

"Weapons launched! This is going to be close, friends!" Helva belts out an ancient folksong accompanied by a driving rhythm and guitar riff that makes me want to sing along—something about whether she should stay or go. The volume fades as if she's leaving audio range.

"Helva! Don't let them capture you." Arun casts a furtive glance over his shoulder at me. "You can't let your code fall into Gagarian hands!"

The song cuts out mid-word. "They don't have a chance." A manic laugh rings out, like an animated evil scientist, then is cut off as the jump countdown reaches zero.

THIRTY-TWO

"Status!" Arun's voice snaps out like a military commander. The rest of us look at each other blankly.

"Who are you asking?" Elodie waves a hand at her blank screens. "Cause I don't have control over anything, and those two are just along for the ride."

"Sorry." Arun swipes his screen. "Raynaud would have—looks like we're back at Sally Ride."

"We jumped directly from Gagarin to S'Ride?" I grab the back of Elodie's seat and lean forward against my restraints. "You can't do that."

"Obviously we can." Arun points at the screen which shows a "Welcome to the Sally Ride system" banner. "Like the jump belts, there's nothing keeping us from doing it except political regulations."

"And the fact that the Gagarin jump beacon shouldn't have Sally Ride in its system." I unbuckle my restraints and stand. "Are you sure we're in the S'Ride System? Maybe it's a fake, to catch defectors."

Arun frowns and swipes through a few screens. "Nope. Unless they've set up a false destination able to mimic S'Ride down to the last emission." He stabs an icon. It flares, then a weird flat tone fills the small bridge. It's followed by ten distinct beeps at different frequencies, and a scratchy, static noise. An electronic tone warbles up and down, cut off by a click. Then Arun's voice speaks: "You have reached the secure connection to Kinduja-net. Please enter your security credentials." Arun's fingers flip through a sequence faster than I can catch, and another banner appears that says, "Welcome, Arun."

"What just happened?" I ask.

"I connected to my virtual network. It's encrypted and transmitted from my office on Sally Ride. There's no way for the Gagarians to mimic that. We're home."

FOR THE NEXT FORTY HOURS, as we make the long, high-speed approach from the jump belt to the planet, we argue about how we ended up in this system. Our conclusion: Helva rigged the coordinates through the Gagarin jump beacon—a risky and theoretically impossible task.

"Maybe not impossible, but it's not something Joe Average could do." Arun runs a hand through his hair as he scans data streaming in front of him.

"Helva is hardly average." I push back from the table, flinging my arms wide as I yawn.

"True." He shoves away the data. "I can't look at this anymore. Did you ever figure out how Risa and Naunet fit into this whole thing?"

Leo straightens his turban. "Risa was part of Grigori's network. Grigori got her assigned to work with Naunet—who knew nothing."

"It was a good cover. I thought Naunet would be more sympathetic to us—since she'd spent some time in the Commonwealth." Elodie leans back in her chair as she strokes the cat. "But how did Grigori know about us? Or rather, about Vanti?"

"Grigori said he heard about me from Gary Banara." I frown. "I thought he was in prison on Kaku."

"Who's Gary Banana?" Elodie bites her lip, but I can see the corners twitch.

I roll my eyes so she knows I noticed. "He went to the academy with me. Then he became a fashion designer, believe it or not. You've heard of Garabana?"

Elodie's mouth forms an O. "He's the one who dressed Kara and Triana for that embassy thing. The one who turned out to be a spy?"

I blink. "The spy part was supposed to be kept quiet, but I suppose Kara told you."

She shrugs. "My daughter tells me everything. But that doesn't mean I share it. I have a great deal of discretion."

Since none of her videos have mentioned Garabana, I can't disagree. "That's true. Anyway, I don't know how Banara got out of prison, but he told Grigori about me. I'd better report that to my superiors. I hope that doesn't mean—" If my identity—and skill set—are known to foreign governments, my usefulness as an undercover operative may have ended. I really don't want that to be the case, but I'll have to wait and see what my handlers say.

"I wonder what happened to Grigori's shuttle." Elodie leans her elbows on the table.

Arun snaps his fingers. "That's right! He and Dima were locked in the cargo hold. With all that food."

"I might have—" Leo stops, eyeing us. We return his gaze. When no one speaks, he goes on. "I might have set the autopilot to take him back to Yussupova. What?" He holds up both hands to ward off our objections. "There was food in there—for kids. And I left him tied up."

"Him and Dima?" Arun pinches the bridge of his nose. "I wonder how Dima will react to being—" He barks out a laugh. "What do you want to bet Grigori's people hold him hostage? He's worth a fortune and has access to the top levels of government. You might have given Grigori the tool to start his revolution."

Leo drops his forehead to the table. "Great."

I pat his arm. "If it's any consolation, Dima definitely deserves it."

"True," Arun agrees.

"I have to admit, the thought of starving children at Yussupova was bothering me a bit. I'm glad they'll get their food." I yawn again. "And if they use Dima to get liberty, I'm okay with that."

Leo pushes back his chair. "I have an announcement." He stands, waiting until all three of us are facing him. "I'm leaving the *Ostelah*. I've accepted a job on Sally Ride. Chez Marcelo is looking for a new pastry chef, and they've offered me the position."

"Leo, no!" Elodie jumps up to grab his arm. "Why are you leaving us?"

"Why?" He stares at her, his jaw slack. "Is getting kidnapped by a crazy man not enough?"

"But I thought you and Grigori were friends?" She drops into her chair.

He chokes out a dry laugh. "He's a pirate—a revolutionary. And he had his minions abduct me! I never met the guy before we got to Gagarin."

"Oh. That's not what he said." Elodie swings her chair back and forth.

Leo shakes his head in disbelief. "Well, if *he* said we're friends—" He rolls his eyes.

I point a finger at him. "You must have liked him a little—you sent him back to his people."

"That was for the kids."

Arun shifts in his chair. "I can see why you'd want to stay planet bound after that. Although after our recent adventure, I'm not planning on heading back to Gagarin any time soon. I'm pretty sure we're persona non grata there. Dima isn't going to be interested in doing business with me after this. If he ever gets away from Grigori."

"I'm sorry," all three of us say at once.

Arun shakes his head and lifts his hands. "Not your fault—any of you. Grigori targeted us, which put us into an untenable position. Why he chose us—" His eyes snap to mine for a brief second, then veer away. "It doesn't matter. The point is, we were in reactive mode—there's no way we could have predicted or avoided most of that. And to be honest, I'm not sure the rewards of that relationship were worth the risks. Dima might be a force for free commerce in Gagarin, but after our meeting, I was having doubts as to whether he was the type of person I wanted to do business with. This makes it easy."

Elodie stifles a yawn and gets to her feet. She got some more time in the med pod since we arrived in system. Her color is better, although she still looks tired. "We've got a few hours before we arrive. I'm going to catch a nap."

I grab her wrist as she passes behind me. "How are you feeling?"

She shrugs. "The med pod says I need a few more hours—and recommended a professional grade model. Which is funny—I thought this one was pro grade?" She glances at Arun.

"It's the best I could buy, but it's a few years old. There are newer models." He shoots a raised brow at me. "If severe injury is likely to be a regular thing, I'll get an upgrade."

I lift both hands. "I'm not planning on regular injuries. But have you seen some of the stuff vid stars do? I think the best med pod credits can buy would be a wise investment." I point at Elodie.

"I can't afford the best." She pauses in the doorway to pick up the cat. "Yet. But we're going to get there!"

Leo waits for Elodie to precede him, then follows her out with a wave. "See you in a few hours."

Arun opens his data file again. Dark circles under his eyes show he's been at this way too long. "I keep going through Helva's data, and I can't..." He shakes his head and pokes another data screen into existence.

I rise and pace around the table. "What is she?" I look around the room, but there's no obvious sign of surveillance, of course. With a flick and a slide, I activate my private jammer. We swept the ship for cams and bugs—and found a dozen placed by the Gagarians as well as some unknown entities. Probably minions of Grigori or Dima or some other would-be capitalist. The last three sweeps came up clean, but I don't trust anyone. "Is she just a good computer simulation of human speech and thought processes? Or is she a sentient—or is it sapient?—being?"

He shoves a hand through his hair again, and it falls limply across his forehead. "I don't know the answer to that. It wasn't my intention to build a self-aware system. And to be clear, it's really hard to tell the difference between a truly self-aware system and one that's really good at mimicking humans. She would say she's capable of independent thought—that's what a human would say, so that's what the system does. But Helva certainly seems to think outside the box."

"You should get some sleep." I put a hand on his shoulder and lean forward to swipe the data away. "It doesn't really matter how she—it—" I break off and start again. "We don't need to figure this out immediately. It's not going to change anything. And there's a good chance we'll never see her again. Even if she escaped, how will she get back to the Commonwealth? Go to bed."

He stands, pressing his hands to his hips and stretching his lower back. His rumpled shirt rides up, displaying a few centimeters of his tight stomach. A little spike of heat goes through me, and I look away.

Straightening, his lips quirk and he reaches out a hand to me. "You wanna come with me? I don't need to *sleep*…"

"You definitely need a shower." I step back. I like Arun, but a physical relationship could complicate our professional one. So I'll play hard to get. For now, at least. I make a shooing motion. "Scoot."

"Scoot?" He yawns as he moves closer, his arms stretching overhead and putting more of his abs on display. "That doesn't seem like a very Vanti thing to say."

I swallow and take another step back. "You don't know me well enough to make that determination."

He smiles lazily. "I've been paying attention, and I've never heard you say 'scoot' before."

I take another step, my heel hitting the compartment bulkhead. "Maybe I'm testing new vocabulary. For my next undercover op."

He moves closer, crowding me against the wall. "Speaking of undercover ops, next time we do one, I'd like a little more advanced notice." He reaches up and taps my nose.

"Did you just boop my nose?" I draw myself up, lifting my chin. My shoulders press against the solid surface behind me. "I am a highly trained security agent. You can't boop my nose."

"I can't?" His index finger moves toward my face.

I grab it in my fist and yank it away. He yelps and jumps back, pulling me with him. I let go so I won't fall into him. "Sorry!"

"That hurt." He flexes his fingers, then shakes his hand. "You aren't very good at non-lethal flirting, are you?"

"I guess not."

"Or you don't want to flirt with me." His eyes narrow as he gives me a closer look. "Are you not interested?"

I glance away, biting my lip. When I look back, he's taken another step away and wears what I think of as his top-lev look. Calm, superior, and in this case, slightly amused. "It's okay. I know how to take 'no' for an answer."

"No, it's not—it's complicated." I turn away, pacing across the room as I speak. "We have a good thing going here." I gesture between him and me, then at the room in general. "Flying with you is the perfect way for Elodie to do her thing, and I don't want to mess that up if things end badly between us."

"You're assuming they'll end badly?" A crack appears in his sophisticated pose, and I see a flicker of sadness. "Why can't they end well?"

I cross my arms. "When does a relationship *ever* end well? It either ends badly or it doesn't end. Even when it's a pre-planned, limited term, non-procreational contract, someone always gets hurt."

He watches me carefully, one brow rising just a fraction.

Is he suggesting we could have a long-term thing? Like a *forever* relationship? That doesn't happen in his social circle. Or mine. At least not very often. I suck in a shaky breath and lift both hands to stop that thought. "Let's just—"

He smiles, the top-lev veneer sliding into place so fast I almost think I imagined that flash of sadness. "Good plan. We'll just. I'm going to grab a shower and hit the hay. See you when we get home." He disappears through the door before I can say anything else.

I suck in another lungful and drop into a chair. *Crisis averted*, I tell myself. Maybe if I say it enough times, it will feel true.

A CALL PINGS ME, breaking me out of a sound, dreamless sleep.

"Vanti." It's Aretha. "Report."

"I sent a report. Didn't you get it?" I sit up, rubbing my eyes. My cabin is dark and warm. I hadn't expected to fall asleep, but I guess recovering from my injuries wore me out.

"I did. You know I like to get an oral report too."

I spend ten minutes going over everything again. I don't think I add anything of value. When I run out of things to say, Aretha waits.

I wait. As long as I can stand. "What?"

Her tone is uncertain, which is unusual for Aretha. "I'm afraid your usefulness might have ended, Vanti."

"No! I can still do my job."

"I'm not questioning your capability. But if Gara Banara is telling random contacts about Vanti's skills, your cover is blown."

"So don't use me as an undercover operative anymore. I can still be useful, even if people know who I am." I listen to her breathe for a few long moments, but I don't say anything. I've learned the best way to win with Aretha is to make my point and wait.

"You'll need a new code name."

I cheer mentally but try to keep my tone even. "It's not like Vanti is particularly secret. It's literally part of my name."

"True. Fine. Your new code name is Dark Quasar. Brilliant but stealthy. I'll throw you in the mix when we need your special skills, but secrecy isn't the highest priority."

"Thank you, Aretha."

"Thank you, Dark Quasar."

I join the others on the flight deck as we approach the planet. Arun sits in the front left seat, with Elodie in the right. Leo and the cat have the seat behind Arun.

Elodie flicks a couple icons. They aren't flight controls, but vid stats. "My numbers are up. Our escape from Gagarin is trending. I might be able to parlay this into a bigger sponsorship."

"You've posted vids?" My hand clamps onto her shoulder. "I'm not in them, am I?"

She gives me a sad, "don't you trust me?" look. "I've kept you off screen. Except for the launch through the glass ceiling—and you're moving too fast for anyone to identify you." She lifts a hand, stalling my interruption. "I scrubbed the meta data, of course. I know the rules. I'm the only one identifiable. I even blurred out Naunet in the early vids. Not that anyone she knows will ever see them."

Arun, Leo, and I all snort.

"You think they will?" Elodie asks hopefully. "Maybe I should have left her in! Her friends will want to see them."

"No, you did right." I fasten my seat restraints. "Her partner tried to kill the secretary general. Poor Naunet is probably in prison right now."

"That's terrible!" Elodie wrings her hands. "You said she didn't know anything."

"Yeah, but the Gagarians won't believe that. There's nothing we can do for her." I shrug, the shoulder straps biting into me. "For all we know, she was working for the government and trying to infiltrate the rebellion."

A comm icon flashes, and a banner appears, indicating the controllers on Station Crippen Hauck request comms. Elodie flicks a virtual switch and chats with them in a low voice while Arun flips through various screens.

"We're cleared for a planetary landing at your runway, Arun." Elodie swipes the comm screen away.

"It's a landing pad, not a runway." Arun throws a map across the forward screen. A red dotted line appears, showing our descent.

"We're landing? I thought with Helva gone we'd dock at the station and take a commercial shuttle." I peer at the map.

Arun shakes his head. "One of the reasons I bought this particular ship was its ability to land. Usually, I'd take the shuttle, but I don't have to. Plus, I want to have my techs go over everything. Doing it dirtside is easier than in a space dock." He sighs softly. "Atmo breach in thirty seconds."

While they flick, swipe, and poke at the interface, I lean back in my seat and close my eyes. The artificial gravity on the *Ostelah* will counteract any forces caused by our descent, but landing is not my favorite part of the trip.

A ping rouses me—an incoming message from an unknown sender pops up. I start to swipe it away but decide I'd better check. My coworkers shouldn't contact me on an unsecured system, but it wouldn't be the first time. I flip the inbound symbol.

"I got away," Helva's voice whispers through my implant. "I'll be back!"

If you enjoyed this story and haven't read the Space Janitor series yet, grab it now!

AUTHOR NOTES

Thanks for reading Dark Quasar Rising. If you liked it, let me know by sending me an email or leaving a review. That way I know if you want more Vanti, Arun, Elodie, and Apollo.

Also, if you go to my webpage, juliahuni.com, you can sign up for my newsletter. That will keep you up to date on my next release, and you'll get access to some free stories.

If you're looking for some more reading, there's a list of all my books on the next page or so.

This book took longer to get out to you readers than I expected. I wrote it in the spring, but things kept getting in the way, not the least of which was my Krimson Empire Kickstarter campaign, and my family's trip to Japan. It's been a dream for many years, and we finally got to celebrate all of the kids' college graduations with a trip to Tokyo, Hakone, Nagoya, Kyoto, and Osaka. Will you see some Japanese influence in future books? You just might.

As always, there are lots of folks to thank. First of all, thanks to my husband who gives me the time, space, and support to write.

AUTHOR NOTES

This book would not have been nearly as good without my editor, Paula Lester of Polaris Editing. Any mistakes you find I probably added after she finished polishing the manuscript. Thanks to my alpha reader, my sister and science fiction author AM Scott. She reads everything I write before anyone else does, and I value her input! Thanks to my amazing beta readers, Anne Kavcic, Barb Collishaw, Jenny Avery, Larry Searing, and Paul Godtland, for finding the little typos that hid and multiplied in the darkness of the computer file, and for making sure I don't leave any gaping plot holes!

Thanks to my sprinting group, Hillary, Paula, AM, Kate, Marcus, and Lou, for keeping me working even when I'd rather be eating cheesecake. Or baking it.

And, of course, thanks to the Big Guy who makes all things possible.

ALSO BY JULIA HUNI

Space Janitor
The Vacuum of Space
The Dust of Kaku
The Trouble with Tinsel
Glitter in the Stars
Sweeping S'Ride
Orbital Operations (a prequel)

Galactic Junk Drawer
(contains Orbital Operations
The Trouble with Tinsel
and Christmas on Kaku)

Tales of a Former Space Janitor
The Rings of Grissom
Planetary Spin Cycle
Waxing the Moon of Lewei
Changing the Speed of Light Bulbs

Friends of a Former Space Janitor
Dark Quasar Rising

Colonial Explorer Corps
The Earth Concurrence
The Grissom Contention
The Saha Declination
The Darenti Paradox

Recycled World

Recycled World

Reduced World

Krimson Empire

Krimson Run

Krimson Spark

Krimson Surge

Krimson Flare

Julia also writes sweet, Earth-bound romantic comedy that won't steam your glasses under the name Lia Huni.

Printed in Great Britain
by Amazon